Glorybound Publishing
Camp Verde, Arizona USA
in the year 2026

The TSOSA PROPHECY

Published by Glorybound Publishing, Camp Verde, AZ
SAN 256-4564
Published in the United States of America
1st Edition
ISBN 978-1-60789-375-2 1-60789-375-4
Copyright data is available on file.
Prochnow, Dale, 1940-
The TSOSA PROPHECY
1. Fiction
I. Title

www.gloryboundpublishing.com

the TSOSA PROPHECY

by
Dale Prochnow

Table of Contents

CHAPTER PAGE

1. A Taste of Defeat 11
2. Above the Planet Atlantae 14
3. San Tomas, New Mexico, U.S.A. 22
4. On Asgaard,
the Third Moon of the Planet Daagar,
in the Beta Reticulæ System 27
5. The Red Shirt 33
6. Deep in the Forest 38
7. Adrift in Space 40
8. The Inglorious Fourth Death of Sub So Ma 45
9. Following the Woman from the Pond 48
10. The Drone Interface 55
11. The Foul Smelling Beast 60
12. Confronting a Threat 64
13. Trapped 68
14. Somewhere in the Gobi Desert 73

CHAPTER PAGE

15. The Awakening 78

16. Penumbra 82

17. Crisis on the Bridge. 89

18. Penumbra in Peril 94

19. Ma Starts a War With the Mar Vin. 97

20. The Boneyard 108

21. A Killing Spree. 113

22. The Door to ReCon is Sealed from the Outside 117

23. Killing Ranjoshiteé. 126

24. The ál Ebon Interface 130

25. Josh Explains the Universe 137

26. Penumbra in the Crosshairs 142

27. The Cobalt Bomb 146

28. The End of the Battle of All Battles 151

Яω (rah)	The master of the universe, eternal, a living deity
Atlantæ	The planet Earth, as known by the followers of Яω Earth, as experienced by a civilization of people who live above the ultra-violet, ultra-sonic areas of human awareness
Яωism	The ethical belief system of the majority of the people of Atlantæ
Cadillac	The avatar of Яω, the enforcer, the punisher, the conjurer (has never been seen in human form)
Tsosa (sō´-sə)	Chosen by Яω to save Atlantæ, The Savior
Ranjoshiteé	A mercenary from the Beta Reticulæ constellation, reputed to have been re-conformed by Яω long before, and in preparation for, the war with ώl Ebon. She reportedly became a warrior in the service of Atlantæ.

Φ

ώl Ebon	The master of the universe, eternal, a living deity
Ebonism	The religion of the entire population of Indus
Indus	The planet Earth, as experienced by a civilization of people who live below the infra-red, infra-sonic areas of human awareness
Ebonites	The people of Indus

Φ

God	The master of the universe, eternal, a living deity A deity shared by numerous religions and cults on planet Earth, some influenced by Яω, others by ἀl Ebon
Earth	The planet Earth, as experienced by those people who live between the infra-red and ultra-violet areas of human awareness
Humans	The people of Earth

Φ

Unibars	The people of the city of Penumbra and the moon, Io
Atlantæns	The followers of Яω who live on Earth, above the ultra-sonic areas of human awareness The majority of the population of the planet Mars The majority of the population of the moon Europa
Titans	The people of the moon Titan

The United Nations Space Corps (UNSC) Military Chain of Command

Roi	Supreme Commander, political Head of State
Sub Roi	Fleet Admiral
So	Commander of any combat ship of the fleet
Sub So	Second in Command of any combat ship of the fleet
	Commander of any support ship of the fleet
	Brigate Area Commander of combat troops
Tau (taw)	Second in Command of combat troops
Sub Tau	Fleet or Combat Line Officer
	Fighter Pilot
Uni Tau	Officer in Training
J Tau	Platoon Level Combat Officer
Chi (chē)	Warrant Officer
Sub Chi	A specialist in communications, tactics, logistics, armaments, materiels, etc.
	Master at Arms
U Chi	Broken down into six levels (or rates), any crew member
	Broken down into six levels (or rates), any combat troops

CHAPTER ONE

SEPTEMBER 2, 2002
A TASTE OF DEFEAT

As the battle raged, the pocket cruiser To was driven farther and farther from the center of action until it had effectively been pushed from its assigned station, impossibly out of position and dangerously close to becoming irrelevant to the outcome of the engagement. At one point, the ship had even come perilously close to being forced into the planet's atmosphere without having previously plotted an entry trajectory or adjusted its shields. Hundreds of the enemy's robotic fighters now filled the space between the To and the ship it was assigned to protect at all costs: the battle cruiser Ja.

For two days, swarms of the crewless attack drones of ál Ebon had hacked away at the To with a single-minded intensity, as though the To itself were the ultimate prize of the battle and not the Ja. This seemed surprising to the commanding officer of the pocket cruiser, because aboard the Ja was the Supreme Commander, Roi Tan, Managing Partner of Atlantæ's World Council and Commander in Chief of the United Nations Space Corps.

The killing or capture of Tan would create a devastating loss for both Atlantæ and the Mars Federation, especially now that her current mission was to convene a conference of government heads, ambassadors and political leaders from Mars, Atlantæ, Europa, Io and Titan in Penumbra, the capital of Atlantæ's only moon, uniting them all against the common enemy, ά́l Ebon. Much was at stake for some of these ancient civilizations. Following centuries of war, several were teetering near the brink of collapse.

After decades of negotiation, an agreement had finally been written, accepted, initialed. With a formal signing, a Union of Solar States would be established and a mighty coalition was within reach. Information, research, raw materials, technological resources, and experience would be shared in an attempt to bring an end to an ill fated war which had grown far beyond the grasp of any one of the member states to win alone.

Later, tariffs would be abolished as inter-system commerce became a reality. Looking ahead, members of the new Union visualized a common commodities market and a shared monetary system, in spite of wide-ranging differences in the political systems and cultures of all the members. Aside from mutual defense, the participants stood to establish an economic entity of great value for their respective civilizations. In the long view, the ability to develop trading partnerships beyond the solar system was the determinate prerequisite for this agreement and everyone was together on this point.

Tan herself was the architect of this powerful alliance.

Atlantæ and the World Council had relied heavily on the strength of Roi Tan for over four hundred years. She had been the one clear voice in an insane, endless war against a tyrannical enemy. Without her leadership, the Council would have crumbled many times. She rallied her followers and made them believe winning was possible: All they needed to do was endure. Her consistent message of freedom at any cost was rousing enough to win re-election again and again. Her do-or-die attitude in the face of the continual attacks on the cities and mounting space corps losses was inspirational to her troops.

Yet, surrender now suddenly seemed entirely possible. The metallic taste of defeat rose in the throat of the commander of the To as she watched the Ja, a once great battle cruiser, come perilously close to being lost and with it, quite probably, an alliance.

Vulnerable and unprotected, the Ja intentionally began to move away from Atlantæ and out into open space. Three of the pocket cruisers in its fleet had been disabled. Adrift, they were left behind to fend for themselves. Sixteen were still in action, but of these, all had been crippled in one way or another. To make matters worse, communications between the Ja and the fleet had been severed hours earlier as the mighty Seventh Fleet of the United Nations Space Corps found itself in a state of retreat.

Only the To remained undamaged.

CHAPTER TWO

SEPTEMBER 3, 2002
ABOVE THE PLANET ATLANTÆ

So Jan, Commander of the To, became maniacally aggressive as her ship was pushed farther and farther from the fleet. Hour after hour, she laid neutron mines and flew back through them at breakneck speed, pulling in the attacking robot drones to their doom, even though it could mean her own destruction. She plotted firing solutions that targeted the To itself with its own laser guided missiles. Calculating the second of impact, the To dodged into the path of a squadron of the attacking drones, only to pull away at the last possible instant. Again and again, she futilely charged toward the Ja, only to be repelled or diverted as the robots efficiently countered her every move toward the stricken battle cruiser.

Dozens of ά l Ebon fighters dogged the pocket cruiser. Then, as if the To's isolation weren't disastrous enough, drone computers had somehow begun jamming the cruiser's command and control communications, countermanding missile firing solutions. In the second day of the battle, Jan's tactics were slowly being nullified.

Although it was the oldest ship of its type, the To was a clone of the most superbly built cruiser in the UNSC fleet. Its computer controlled the latest tactical, armaments, and defensive capabilities.

The ship's maneuverability, holographic projectability and capacity to cruise in refracted light and alternate dimensions was state-of-the-art. The forty members of the crew had fought together, in harmony, for over two hundred years. The To's commander was a four hundred year veteran of the ál Ebon war. In addition, So Jan, many times winner of the coveted Blue Battle Cross for Valor, was the Space Corp's most trusted, most decorated commander.

At the moment, Jan was alone on the bridge with her navigator and one guard. Her second in command, Sub So Ma, had gone to CenCon moments earlier to determine if there were tactical or firing solutions which could not be overridden by the enemy. Jan studied the holographic battle projector, observing that the bulk of the ál Ebon battle drones seemed to be massing between her ship and the Ja. The battle cruiser appeared to be relatively free from attack at the moment.

"We have been intentionally driven from the Ja," Jan thought. *"Why?"*

"Computer," she asked, "what is the current tactical situation?"

"No casualties, no structural damage," the computer reported. "All laser guided missiles are armed. All photo rifles are locked on their assigned targets. All remaining neutron mines are armed and in firing position."

"Then why are we not firing?" Jan asked incredulously.

"New firing codes have been entered."

"Explain."

"All previous firing sequences have been overridden."

"For what reason?"

"Alternative targets have been assigned."

"Identify the new targets."

"The battle cruiser Ja and the pocket cruisers Te, Ja and Corju."

"What?"

"The To will re-enter the battle in thirty-seven seconds," the computer reported.

"Belay that command."

"I cannot."

"Belay that command!"

The computer remained silent.

"Who has overwritten the codes?" Jan demanded.

"Sub So Ma."

"How is this possible?"

"Sub So Ma has been assigned command of this ship."

"By whose authority?"

"The computer does not know," the computer reported.

"Where is Sub So Ma at this moment?"

"Sub So Ma is en route to the bridge."

"Computer, am I still in command on this vessel?" Jan asked.

"For approximately thirty-two seconds," the computer reported.

"Computer, enter Atlantæ's atmosphere on my command."

"The computer has not directed the ship's shields properly for a command of this nature," the computer reported. "No trajectory has been plotted for this maneuver. There is a one hundred percent probability the helm will lose control during atmospheric penetration without a pitch solution. There is a ninety-eight percent probability that the ship will break apart upon entering the atmosphere without a guidance solution. There is a ninety-four percent probability the ship will crash into the surface of the planet without a landing solution. There is a ninety-thre…"

With a burst, Sub So Ma entered the bridge, her weapon drawn.

"Computer," So Jan commanded, snapping her command-seat battle security belt into place, "Enter!"

Violently, the To changed course, heading straight toward the planet. The ship crashed into the hard outer shell of the atmosphere just as Ma fired her weapon, causing her to miss. For one second the weapon sang a familiar whine as it recharged. When the charge light came on, Ma aimed her weapon at Jan once more and pushed the firing mechanism, missing again as the craft began to tumble.

"Adjust the shields," Jan screamed.

"Sub So Ma is now in command of this vessel," the computer reported.

"Ma," Jan commanded. "Adjust the shields."

"Go to hell," Ma snarled as she was thrown against the NavCom station and then against a bulkhead.

"What do you think you are doing?" Jan demanded.

"I've taken over the ship," Ma said as she checked to see if her weapon had recharged.

"You?" Jan asked incredulously. "Adjust the shields," she commanded.

"We can all die," Ma said. "My mission has been completed."

"Just what is your mission, Sub So Ma?" Jan asked sarcastically.

"To prevent you from protecting the Tsosa," Ma replied with a smirk.

“The Tsosa prophecy is a myth!”

“No. It is not.”

“My being born to protect the Tsosa is myth!” Jan screamed.

“No,”

“Computer,” Jan screamed, “override all previous commands from Sub So Ma. Refer to Red Battle Code 75-201 of the Council of Military High Command on mutiny. Number c-125, Paragraph 7, Sub set (a). Return the helm to my command. Plot a trajectory. Adjust the shields.”

Immediately the tumbling stopped as the cruiser altered course.

When she could control her weapon, the bridge guard fired her laser at Ma, disrupting the neural pathways to the Sub So’s hand and arm, and dislodging her weapon.

“There is a seventy-four percent probability the ship will crash without a landing solution. Seventy-eight. Eighty-one. Eighty-fo…” the computer began reporting.

“Computer,” So Jan said, “Plot a landing solution and implement.”

Again the cruiser altered course.

“Two hundred and twenty-seven robot fighters have entered the atmosphere in pursuit of this vessel,” the computer reported.

“Ha!” Ma exclaimed.

“Computer,” Jan said, “plot a masking reconfiguration solution to conform with the spectrum of light between ultra-violet and infrared.”

“Spectral reconfiguration solution plotted,” the computer reported one second later.

"Computer, alter the ship's spectral configuration."

The ambient light on the bridge immediately made a subtle change from violet to azure.

"Oh, my God, you're tricky!" Ma screamed in exasperation.

She charged Jan, who was now standing alongside her command seat, driving them both into the NavCom station. The bridge guard fired at Ma once more, but hit Jan instead, knocking her unconscious. The guard's weapon began to recharge immediately. Ma made a rolling dive for her weapon and came up standing on the far side of the bridge, firing directly at the guard.

The guard died just as the light on her weapon came on.

"Now," Ma snarled, "as for you." Her laser came down on the unconscious Jan.

At that moment, the ship reached the surface of the planet, clipping a tree at the top of a mountain in its descent, and slamming headlong into a forest below.

Everyone on the craft was knocked unconscious as the To came violently to rest against the side of a mountain in the state of New Mexico. Those in the forward compartments were killed outright. Others began to die more slowly as they silently bled out their lives onto compartment floors throughout the ship.

The ship remained silent except for the computer.

"The vessel is at rest on the surface of the planet," it reported. "There is a one hundred percent probability that everyone is dead in the forward missile compartments. There is a ninety-seven percent probability that everyone is dead in the forward crew's quarters. There is a…" the computer droned on.

Fortunately, the computer had plotted a landing solution.

Jan was the first to regain consciousness. Disoriented, she moved to the escape hatch and pressed the release mechanism, stepping outside the craft as the door was still opening. Without a backward glance, she stumbled across one of the forward nacelles and dropped into the forest.

She had traveled about a half a mile, climbing a small ridge and descending the far side into a large grove of aspen trees when she began to regain her cognitive abilities. Fully awakened from her confused fog but struggling to think clearly, she found herself standing in the middle of what looked like a very small, very cold lake.

Jan became aware that Ma had appeared, carrying a fully charged weapon in her good hand. Ma, still in somewhat of a stupor from the crash, had with superhuman effort, acted once more to complete her mission, following her commander through the forest, with every intention of killing her. Now, standing less than ten feet away, at the edge of a clear pool, in the heart of a strange wilderness, she raised her weapon to a person who had been her friend and mentor for hundreds of years.

"The Tsosa prophecy is a myth!" Jan spat in frustration. "Myth," she whispered.

"The Tsosa will come into being today," Ma said dispassionately.

"And, how do you know this?"

"I am in communication with ά̇l Ebon."

"You? An agent? I don't believe it!"

"Believe."

For long moments, Jan awaited the moment of her death in a state of frustration. When she finally spoke, her voice was filled with conciliation. "Listen, it's true I was re-conformed by the Яω," she said. "But that was over four hundred years ago – before the war.

During all the years since, nothing has ever demonstrated to me that the Tsosa prophecy was real. Nothing! I've never been instructed to do anything. I have only been a warrior for the Council. That is my only calling. Яω has never reappeared to me. For all I know, he does not exist anymore. For all I know, he is a myth."

"Then it's true. You were Ranjoshiteé."

"Once, yes."

"Prepare to die."

"Ma, we are friends!"

"No," Ma said, "and you are the enemy of all humanity. The Tsosa will be the end of civilization as we have known it. Neither one of you can be allowed to live." Her weapon, with the setting light on kill, was aimed once more.

Without warning, a terrible crash sounded from over the shoulder of Jan. In a horrifying instant, Ma was thrown violently backwards, smashing against the ground: A gigantic hole suddenly appearing in her chest. She lay on her back, in soft grass, gasping until she died, blood from her body spilling softly into the dark earth.

Her eyes betrayed the surprise of her last moment of life.

CHAPTER THREE

SEPTEMBER 3, 2002
SAN TOMAS, NEW MEXICO, U.S.A.

Marvin T. Jarvin was asleep. His children sat close by, waiting patiently until he woke. His wife was visiting her sister in Snowflake, Arizona, and he was in charge of the family until her return. Marvin T. Jarvin was dreaming: His nose twitched, his eyes rolled violently, his right foot peddled madly and he hooted or snorted every once in a while.

Stonie, his son of six, laughed at these antics. Seated next to his father's elbow, he rolled backward and covered his mouth with glee.

"It's not funny," Clementine said sternly. Stonie's older sister was seven and had memorized all the rules. Clementine never broke any of the rules. She carefully covered her small knees with the thin cloth of her dress: Her tiny feet doubled back beneath her bottom. Her top teeth rested on a thin, pale lower lip. On the floor, she sat as close to her father as she could without touching him.

"Ha, ha, ha," her younger brother boomed loudly, pointing to his father's leg. Deftly, the boy lifted a crumbling peanut butter sandwich from the floor and took a prodigious bite. "Ha, ha, ha," he yelled through the mouthful. It came out something like, "Jaa, jaa, jaa." With great care, he placed the sandwich back on the dirty linoleum, licking his fingers.

"You're gonna wake him," Clementine threatened.

"He has'ta wake up sometime," Stonie muttered.

"What?" Marvin said groggily.

"See!" Clementine whispered officiously.

The sleeping man was rather short, with a barrel of a chest which rose above the floor like a mountain and with arms as thick as most men's thighs. No living man could put his hands all the way around Stonie's father's neck. Building muscle upon muscle, Marvin had worked in the quarry since he was seven. Stonie's grandfather had opened the mine when Marvin was still in diapers. The entire family had dug and polished quartz ever since, making clocks and book ends and soap dishes and things like that, for the department stores in Albuquerque and Santa Fe. Three generations (none had ever gone to school) had made a living off the polished stone.

It was hard, but they did it together.

When his father died, Marvin kept right on digging and polishing. He didn't even go to the funeral. It wasn't really a funeral. A pine box, a pauper's plot, and no one to say the words as two strangers lowered the wooden box into a hole and covered it up. That's all.

Later, Marvin placed a beautiful, polished quartz stone at his father's head. "Marvin O. Jarvin" was all that had been carved into it because the son did not know the date of his father's birth, nor even his middle name.

As a matter of fact, his father's entire name had been invented. Marvin O. Jarvin had been born in an insane asylum in Indiana.

He had been given no name. Marvin's father's name had come into being on his eighth birthday, the day he ran away. "Marvin Jarvin," he had said, "I can remember that."

Until the coming year, when the law and the social workers would force Stonie into school, the boy spent his days in the quarry beside his father. Even at his young age, Stonie's hands were leather hard and rough, cracked and callused. Stonie could make a muscle that was the envy of a grown man. He could work, undaunted, for hours.

Stonie could do anything for hours. Just now, for instance, the boy had waited patiently beside his father, a man who had drifted into a deep sleep following the seizure he had suffered at dusk the previous evening. All through the night, Stonie made sure his father did not swallow his tongue. It was his job. And Stonie always did his job. Just like his sister, he followed the rules. Now he could relax as Marvin slept, even enjoy his father's flailing leg.

Marvin looked like their dog, Stonie thought, chasing a cat in his sleep. The boy put his hand to his mouth and giggled. He loved his father.

With an unexpected burst, sunrise cast a brilliantly mote-spotted, orange shaft of light through a nearby window, suffusing the room in a warm glow.

"I should wake him," Stonie said immediately.

"No!" Clementine cried urgently, rising to her feet for emphasis.

"He has to get the meat, Clementine."

"But, he's been sick."

"He's all right," Stonie said, "I think."

"What if he gets sick again while hunting? What if he swallows his tongue? What if you're not there to help him? What if he...?"

"He can count cities like he always does, Clementine," Stonie interrupted importantly. "He can…"

"That doesn't always work."

"He'll be all right."

"Don't," Clementine begged.

Ignoring his sister, Stonie moved his father's powerful shoulder. "Dad," he said into Marvin's ear.

"Mobile, Natchez, Oklahoma City, Peoria, Quinc…" Marvin began counting right where he had stopped when he passed out the previous night.

"You're okay, dad," Stonie said soothingly.

"It's all over, daddy," Clementine caressed reassuringly, bending over her father's face. Her hair fell onto the man's broad, flat nose and it twitched.

"You've gotta get the meat, dad," Stonie said. "Remember?"

"Racine," Marvin continued drunkenly. "Santa Ana, Tulsa…"

"It's okay," Stonie said.

"God, I'm hungry," Marvin said suddenly. His eyes opened.

"You can have what's left of my sandwich," Stonie coaxed.

Remaining on his back, Marvin took a big bite of the peanut butter sandwich. "Goog," he said around a mouthful.

"I feel good," Marvin said at last. "What time is it?"

"About five-thirty," Stonie replied.

"Ohmygosh," Marvin said, "I gotta get the meat."

"I told you," Stonie said to Clementine.

Marvin rolled onto his knees and put one foot on the floor. "Where's my shooter," he said to no one in particular.

Clementine turned and went to a small broom closet in the corner of the kitchen, where she retrieved Marvin's heavy weapon and returned to her father's side just as he was finally standing. Without a word, Marvin grabbed the piece and walked through the door of the dilapidated trailer which was their home, down three steps to the blacktop and one step to the gate.

"Stay inside 'til I get back," he instructed, gently pushing the rusted pipe of a gate back into its tilted place of rest against the broken post.

CHAPTER FOUR

JANUARY 12, 1552
ON ASGAARD, THE THIRD MOON OF THE PLANET DAAGAR, IN THE BETA RETICULAE SYSTEM

Яω commanded a meeting with Ranjoshiteé in this strange place. Ranjoshiteé sat cross-legged in the early morning light of the first risen sun. She tried (for effect) to look patient, but her belly quivered with a terror she felt inside but could not describe. Her eyes surveilled separately as she carefully considered the vast, abandoned garbage dump before her.

Ranjoshiteé's rich black eyebrows remained furrowed. They were streaked with long white spikes and clung haphazardly to the edge of her broad, sloping forehead, looking very much like fat caterpillars brushed from a leaf of a juicy calloberry bush. They wiggled continually. Beneath the caterpillars, thick blue lids folded across her small black eyes and wet, coarse black hair shot from deep within the pores of her cheeks and from her neck. Her hair hid (almost) the ancient blue tattoo, which blurred her clammy skin, as it cascaded in sticky curls across her fat breasts and down her thick shoulders.

Ranjoshiteé remained cross-legged, pretending to meditate.

"Oohoooolum," she intoned majestically. Ranjoshiteé had

always loved the sound of her own voice. It resonated like a taut bow across the gut string of an ancient violetta.

Below her, a ringed rodent's tail protruded from a crumpled box at the base of her carefully selected tall black rock. It seemed to flick impatiently each time she repeated a mantra. While one of Ranjoshiteé's shiny eyes perused the rotten mounds for the slightest portent of danger, the other remained focused on the long, white, hairless thing that languished so innocently in the box, in the morning fog. The elfin woman pointed a fat, jointed finger at the tail as if to accuse it of something.

"You act like you can hear me," she mused under her breath.

The tail remained still.

"Oooohoooooollummm..." Ranjoshiteé boomed again, with a weather-eye out for the twitch. Stretching out the mantra, she gave the creature every opportunity to respond.

"There, you did it again!" Ranjoshiteé cried in triumph, slapping her fat thigh, forgetting her original terror.

"What did I do?" a reedy voice responded from deep within the box.

Ranjoshiteé, startled, nearly fell from the rock.

The rat did not speak again, and Ranjoshiteé fidgeted. Then, quite unconvincingly, she pretended to ignore the voice. Nervously, she started her mantra once more. "Oooohoo..."

"Well?" the thin voice shot.

Ranjoshiteé's legs began to quake. "...ooooollummmm," she continued shakily.

One eye darted back and forth across the face of the box for her tormentor.

The tail disappeared into the box with a snap.

Ranjoshiteé jumped in her skin. Both of her eyes stared as one into the rectangular black hole.

"I hate that!" Ranjoshiteé whispered, suddenly wanting desperately to flee to the quiet of her enormous, cluttered cave.

"If Яω were here," the thin voice said suddenly, "you would answer my question."

"Яω?" Ranjoshiteé gasped, searching the mounds desperately.

"Don't make me come out of this box," the thin voice cried.

"I knew it!" Ranjoshiteé whined, thinking the tail was probably one of Яω's disguises.

At that moment, a thin wind whistled through the aromas of Ranjoshiteé's beard, stirring the caterpillars on her forehead. She tore her eyes from the box. Something powerful pulled her attention to a distant mound upon which stood a solitary figure, shrouded by morning, cloaked in an enormous black cape and protected by a stunted black dingo.

"*Ranjoshiteé,*" a mellow voice suddenly cooed within her head.

"Яω," Ranjoshiteé whispered in awe with the wonderful voice still ringing in her mind. The voice was serene and rich, caressingly soft...friendly...but commanding.

"*Cadillac,*" the voice suddenly demanded, "*come out of that box!*"

The tail, which until now had languished in the door of the box, twitched violently. It seemed to glow in the ambient light of the first of the two rising suns. The creature, however, remained inside its conscripted, cardboard carapace.

"Cadillac?" Ranjoshiteé echoed. "The conjurer?" Shivers crawled along the inside of her fat leg.

"Yes, Cadillac!" the voice inside the box snapped, disgustedly.

"*Cadillac*," the voice inside Ranjoshiteé's head demanded a second time.

"Whom did you expect?" Cadillac said importantly to Ranjoshiteé, ignoring the demand of the voice from the distant mound.

Ranjoshiteé was completely unable to answer.

You see, Ranjoshiteé *was* a creature of fear... *driven* by fear. After two hundred and seventy three years, though she may have learned to hide it from others, she was nonetheless a creature of fear. Sometimes, the fear made her strong. At least she could always act in her own enlightened self-interest. At least she understood the motivations behind her decisions. But at this moment, Ranjoshiteé knew that this particular fear made it impossible for her to do anything. She was frozen.

"*Perhaps the tail belongs to Яω*," she thought.

And now she knew. If this were really Яω before her – the One, the master of the universe – she was doomed. Was it already too late? Why would Яω act in such a stealthy manner, unless he was planning to kill her? Had Яω been inside the box all along? Ranjoshiteé trembled around her short, stunted bones. A line of drool descended to her breast.

"*So what, if I only act out of fear*," Ranjoshiteé thought defensively. "*I'm still alive, aren't I?*" Suddenly she was bolstered by the fact that nothing really had had happened to her in two hundred and seventy three years.

Just as suddenly, she knew the rationalization was irrelevant. Яω had commanded her to be here. Why? It was not for nothing that Яω was depicted in the art of so many worlds as the hooded cobra. What did he want?"

And now, if this was really Cadillac in the box – the Conjurer, the torturer of Phobos and Deimos (and no one knew how many other civilizations), she was doomed. Яω and Cadillac, Cadillac and Яω: Ranjoshiteé's mind swam.

From inside Ranjoshiteé's head, Яω's voice began to coax. *"If you are so afraid, little woman, why have you come?"*

"Yes, why?" echoed Cadillac, from deep within the box.

In terror, Ranjoshiteé fixed one eye on the mound, the other on the box.

"Was it fear of fear that brought you?" Cadillac sneered.

A pink, whiskered nose pointed out from the box, as if to give emphasis to the question. Ranjoshiteé stared again at the rat, with both eyes fixed on the nose. She gulped. So enraptured by her proximity to Cadillac, she did not realize the figure from the mound had moved to within a foot of her elbow. The dingo began to relieve itself on the dwarf's leg.

"Ranjoshiteé," the figure said quietly. "I have chosen you to represent me."

As the dwarf stood in awe, Яω placed a heavy hand on her shoulder. "You may be cunning and pragmatic, even mercenary," Яω said, "but you are a good soul: intrepid, inventive and inherently kind." He spoke softly.

His voice was filled with love.

"From this moment, you will continually be in danger and you will die many times, my friend, sometimes very painfully. But you will live, as well. Live as no one has ever lived. The fear you have experienced until now is nothing to the fear you will endure in the future, but you will always prevail. You will also know joy and victory. You have proved this to me many, many times. Yes, you are the one. You are the only one to carry this mission successfully to its conclusion.

"As of today, you will no longer be Ranjoshiteé. You will become a new being: A warrior. As this being, you will have but one mission, to defend the Tsosa when he comes into being."

The voice once again spoke to Ranjoshiteé's mind.

"Cadillac will instruct you."

Ranjoshiteé's eyes shone with awe.

"We will meet again. Until then, live well, my little friend."

The figure disappeared and the dingo trotted out into the dump and rounded a mound of refuse and was gone.

CHAPTER FIVE

SEPTEMBER 3, 2002
THE RED SHIRT

"Marvin Jarvin!" Lamont Larsen said in a loud voice, as Marvin entered a small general store dedicated to hunting and fishing in the little town of San Tomas in northern New Mexico. "You're getting a late start aren't you? Hunting season began when the sun came up this morning. Everybody is out there ahead of you." Lamont winked broadly to his brother Jay, who was absently leaning against the counter by the open cash register, pushing pennies around inside the drawer with his finger.

Several hunters who were also getting a late start, milled about the room.

Jay pushed the cash drawer closed with his thumbs and leaned on his elbows. "Yeah," he said, "You're so late, someone might think you're a deer and shoot you when you walk up."

Someone chuckled.

"I'm a man, Jay." Marvin said good-naturedly. "I'm not a deer."

"But, you look like a deer," Jay said, "You're all brown. You've gotta be red, Marvin. You've gotta be red. Isn't that right Lamont?"

"Gotta be red," Lamont echoed. "No doubt about it."

"How?" Marvin queried.

"A red shirt, Marvin. You gotta have a red shirt. Pretty simple, huh?"

"I don't have one," Marvin said. "I'll just have to go without."

"Nope. Nope," Lamont said. "Have one right here."

From beneath a counter, Lamont produced a huge, dusty red flannel shirt. He did not shake away the grime, just held it into the air by the shoulders. "Here we go, Marvin," he said happily. "Just the ticket."

"Can't afford no red shirt," Marvin said. "Not one good as that, anyway."

"Oh, but you can," Lamont said.

"No," Marvin said. "I gotta buy shells. I don't have money for no shirt.

"The law says you have to have a red shirt, Marvin."

"The heck with the law," Marvin said.

"C'mon," Lamont said, "Don't get mental on me."

"I just wanna buy six shells." Marvin was suddenly angry. "Don't have no money for no shirt, and that's that. Stop teasing me. Lamont, you shouldn't make jokes about mental problems." Marvin was quiet for a moment. "I could hurt you, Lamont," he said patiently.

"Six!" Jay yelled from across the room, breaking the mood. "You can't just buy six. You have to buy a whole box. That's the rules. I can't break a box, and that's it."

"You know the rules," Lamont repeated, trying not to laugh.

"You have a broken box, Lamont, and you know it."

"What are you talking about?"

"That .30-06 Winchester you sold last week," Marvin said. "You traded for a .303 Enfield just like mine. And you got a half a box of shells, too. I saw the whole thing when I got my hunting license."

"You don't miss a trick, do you," Lamont said.

"No."

"Okay, suppose I sell you the broken box. What about the shirt?"

Marvin doggedly shook his head.

"Marvin?"

Again, Marvin shook his head. This time he frowned. He felt himself getting upset again. He began counting cities under his breath to remain calm.

"It's the law," Jay said from the other side of the store. "Red. That's it."

"But, I don't have the money..."

"You've got good credit," Lamont interrupted. "We'll put it on your tab."

"That's for food, and you know it, Lamont."

"Well, you're hunting for food today, aren't you?"

"I suppose."

"Then the cost of the shirt belongs on your food bill, doesn't it?"

"I suppose."

"Well, there you go."

Lamont stepped behind Marvin and offered the shirt. "Try it on," he coaxed.

Marvin pushed a ham-like hand into one sleeve while Lamont held onto the collar with all his might. Marvin wriggled and grunted and Lamont pushed until, finally, they had gotten him into the shirt. The trouble was that the material had become a wad behind Marvin's neck, and his arms were unable to hang naturally at his side. From any angle, a person could not see that Marvin was wearing a red shirt, except from the back, where it was bunched up around his neck. His enormous body looked terribly uncomfortable with his arms stuck high in the air.

Lamont sniggered.

"It doesn't fit too well," Marvin admitted.

"No problem," Lamont said, retrieving a pair of scissors from the counter. Without comment, he cut up the middle of the back of the shirt, nearly to the collar. He then cut down into the sleeves from the back until Marvin was able to lower his arms.

"There," Lamont said smugly.

Moving to the front, he pulled the shirt across Marvin's chest and buttoned every button, except the three he left open at the neck. "And we'll just put the whole thing on your bill," he said as he worked.

At last, he took Marvin by the arm to a mirror at the back of the store.

"What do you think?" Lamont said.

"I can't pay for it all at once," Marvin said.

"No problem," Lamont said, walking Marvin to the front counter. Jay had already placed a crushed box of .303 ammo next to the register. It was so old, one could hardly read the label. Jay began adding the price of the shirt to Marvin's tab.

"That'll be eight dollars for the ammo," he said, smiling.

Marvin produced a wad of crumpled one-dollar bills, counting painfully.

"And, that'll be twenty-four dollars for the shirt," Jay added, sliding the tab across the counter for Marvin to sign.

With some effort, Marvin placed his "X" on the paper, carefully studying the account balance when he had finished. It had more than doubled with one entry. He quietly walked from the store, turning abruptly in the doorway.

"Thanks, Lamont," he said and disappeared around the corner.

Everyone in the store exploded in laughter.

"You're a bastard," Jay said finally.

"Ain't I?"

CHAPTER SIX

SEPTEMBER 3, 2002
DEEP IN THE FOREST

It was still quite dark on the northern side of the mountain when Marvin arrived. He parked his rickety International Scout next to a juniper thicket and quickly climbed about a mile and a half up the fern encrusted mountainside. By eight forty five he was in place, in a tree, in the blind he had carefully constructed years before. Above and to his left, the mountain cast a long shadow across the forest. Sunlight had broken across the top three hours earlier. Marvin sighed. He believed he had gotten to his hiding place in time, in spite of the late hour.

Below and to his right, a tiny cattle tank nestled into the trees. A small herd of deer, on a regular schedule, would arrive soon to slake its thirst with a chilly morning drink and he intended to shoot one of them.

A rancher had built this water catchment many years ago but never used it. Ignored by the rancher's children and unknown to the company which had purchased the property from his grand-children fifty years later, the tiny reservoir lay like gossamer silk beneath the branches of an old oak tree. Mist rose from exposed roots, buried in the middle of a whistling aspen grove. Mosquitoes from above, and tadpoles from below, roiled the surface until the water shimmered happily in the early morning light. A blue jay flitted down for a quick sip. He craned his beak high into the air; a porcupine grumbled in; a squirrel flicked his tail and scampered from his tree.

Marvin's world was at peace.

As important as it was to remain awake, he soon drifted off to sleep.

CHAPTER SEVEN

SEPTEMBER 2, 2002
ADRIFT IN SPACE

Roi Tan listened in disbelief to the computer of the UNSC Battle Cruiser Ja as it reported, in detail, the losses suffered by the fleet during the previous forty-eight hour period. Not only had the vaunted United Nations Seventh Fleet been driven to the edge of defeat in a particularly vicious battle with the ά1 Ebon robot drones, but it had been forced from Atlantæ's orbit, retreating into open space, vulnerable and unprotected. In the process, the Seventh Fleet had left behind four indispensable pocket cruisers, the Te, Ja, Corju and To.

The first three were adrift in orbit around Atlantæ. With communications down, it was impossible to know the status of these ships or their crews. Now that the fleet had pulled away, it was likely that the robot drones would destroy them unless their commanders could find cover, and that seemed unlikely.

The To had been driven back to the surface of the planet. The commander of the Set reported that her battle projector had displayed the disappearance of a ship near the surface and presumed it to be the To. In any event, the To had not been recorded by the Ja's holographic battle projector since sixteen thirty-four. There had been no communication with So Jan's pocket cruiser for over ten hours. It was now feared that every person on the To had been lost. It might not be possible to find them in time to re-conform the dead. In any event, no search would be implemented until the fleet returned. When that would be, was unknown.

From behind the half-mile long observation windows of the bridge, Tan could see down into the cavernous interior of the Ja. Every second or two an emergency vehicle could be seen ferrying the wounded or transporting supplies, machines, or equipment through the interior biosphere. A frenzied determination to repair the ship gripped the officers and crew and they worked tirelessly to return her to combat readiness.

Monotonously, the computer continued to report on the condition of the fleet. Every remaining cruiser had been damaged, it reported, some severely, including the Ja itself. Ship to ship communications were down, but since the disappearance of the To, the battle seemed to have abated. Hundreds of the robot drones had entered Atlantæ's atmosphere when she went down. It didn't seem likely that they were hunting solely for the To, but anything was possible.

During the lull in the battle, communications officers were doing everything possible to re-establish intra-fleet computer links. In the meantime, a few of the fleet's pocket cruiser dispatch launches had been deployed to facilitate a kind of "runner system" of communications. Fleet commanders were now desperately using the downtime to get beyond the short-range scanning capabilities of the ál Ebon drones.

"Four hundred and twelve corsairs and their pilots have been lost," the computer droned on. "One thousan..." It was obvious that Tan was not listening to the report. She turned, at last, to the fleet commander. "Sub Roi Bon, we must make Penumbra in time for the signing," she said.

"Not with the fleet in this condition," Bon answered.

"Leave the fleet. Go it alone."

"Too risky. No. I don't recommend it."

"How long would it take the Fifth Fleet to reach us?"

"Seven hours. But we are not in communication with Sub Roi Watt. She does not yet know we need help. So a seven hour countdown really begins the moment the Fifth sets sail."

"What's the downside if we wait?"

"We get caught in the open. ál Ebon would like nothing better than to catch you without the protection of a functioning fleet. They would love to destroy this ship, or capture it, with you on board."

"What's the downside if we go?"

"We get caught in the open."

"But the positive side is that we have a chance to get the pact signed," Tan said. "If we're late, or don't arrive altogether, the treaty may never be ratified."

"A treaty can always be ratified, Roi Tan," Bon said.

"No, this time there's too much at stake. If some of the pocket cruisers can go with us, all the better. If not, we go alone."

"Roi, I…"

"Your objection is noted, Sub Roi. Make it happen."

The Supreme Commander left the bridge.

"Computer," the Sub Roi said, "plot a Penumbra vector solution for the Ja." She turned to the commander of the ship. "How many pocket cruisers can we expect to take with us?" she asked.

"You'll have my report within the hour," the So responded.

In her quarters, Tan brooded over the loss of the To and its battle hardened commander. It was inconceivable that Яω could have abandoned such an important symbol of strength as So Jan.

It was as if he were ceding Atlantæ itself.

The war had turned unpredictably ugly in recent years. ál Ebon was becoming more powerful every day – to the point of challenging the World Council for supremacy in the solar system. His pilot-less fleets now attacked in overwhelming numbers. They seemed invincible. Once they would have been flicked away like so many dung flies: Now they attacked with impunity. Yesterday's losses to the once outmatched drone hordes were proof enough.

Worse, to Tan, was the loss of So Jan. A puzzling loss: Hadn't Jan been given a lifetime assignment by Яω himself? How was it possible to cast aside such a forceful beacon of hope at the height of her power? Had her mission been abandoned?

"Perhaps the Tsosa prophesy has been a myth after all," Tan thought.

She had known Jan for over three hundred years. She had been aware of the prophecy for nearly as long.

The first time they met was on the tarmac, in the biosphere of the battle cruiser Nopar near the end of the sixteenth century. They had stood beside a squadron of corsairs, one of which was piloted by the then Sub Tau Jan.

Tan had been startled by Jan's physical appearance. At five foot four, the young warrior was a giant among her peers. She towered six inches above the tallest of the other officers who had been assembled to receive the Blue Battle Cross for Valor. In addition, her uniform did not disguise the normally androgynous frame of a warrior-officer. This young pilot could have easily been a throw-back to when women suckled babies, she was so full-breasted.

In another break from standard, Jan had insisted on keeping her hair long, barely within regulations. A lightly twisted braid from each side of her head had been loosely woven into the hair at her back, holding the flaming mass in check. Everything had been tied at the nape of her neck. Her appearance was formidable above that deadly serious face. *"I would hate to be your enemy,"* Tan had thought.

"Your citation does not mention that you have been recommended four times previously for this award," Tan had said, looking directly into the warrior's (one) brown and (one) blue-green eyes.

"I have not been sent here to win awards for valor," Jan had answered simply.

"Sent?" Tan had puzzled aloud. "Win awards? Our world is at war, Sub Tau. Perhaps we might discuss your choice of words some other time," Tan had uttered condescendingly.

"Perhaps," Sub Tau Jan had replied.

Not an auspicious beginning perhaps, but on their second meeting Jan would save Roi Tan's life and earn a fifth palm leaf for her Blue Battle Cross. In that moment, the two were bonded together forever. Roi Tan, leader of the World Council and Sub Tau Jan, fighter pilot, formed a lasting friendship in spite of the differences in their stations.

With a heavy heart, Tan now left the To behind.

At 21:41 hours on the third of September 2002, the battle cruiser Ja and nine pocket cruisers began a twenty-five hour run for the backside of the moon. At the time of their departure, communications between the Ja and the ships of her small fleet had still not been re-established. And the Ja was still badly wounded.

CHAPTER EIGHT

SEPTEMBER 3, 2002
THE INGLORIOUS FOURTH DEATH OF SUB SO MA

So Jan remained rooted to the bottom of the pond for what seemed like an eternity, looking at the body of her dead friend, struggling to interpret the events of the last few moments, trying to comprehend the brutality of Ma's killing. *"What could have done this?"* she wondered.

She was unaware that another being had entered the water, or that it had begun moving toward and directly behind her. Thin ripples moved outwardly, ahead of the surging creature, caressing her thighs and moving on to expend themselves on the edge of the pond, but she could not see them. After a time, she heard a noise or felt a presence and turned to confront a Neanderthal mountain of a creature, disheveled, foul smelling and, strangely, in tears.

Although clothed, the monster seemed aboriginal in nature. He spoke haltingly, in an unfamiliar, uncultured tongue, guttural and harsh to her ears. The voice alone was frightening, filled with a deep timbre, unlike the voice of any male whom she had ever known. Muddy-brown in color, his face, broad and flat, was irregular and unrefined. His eyes were dull, reflecting a mind incapable of communicating the least sophisticated concept. His shoulders and neck were massive, unlike Atlantæn males, who were small in stature, smooth of skin, and clean, with a soft, cultured musculature.

The brute lumbered through the water, carrying a long metal and wooden stick as though it were a gift. Jan backed away, aware that she might be in a new and more serious danger. *"Could this be an avatar of ál Ebon?"* she thought. *"Was this creature here to assist Ma in the killing of the protector of the Tsosa?"* Jan's mind whirled.

When he was close enough, Jan instinctively swatted away the metal stick. It splashed noisily into the water and neither of them looked to see where it landed. *"I have not trained to confront a being this large,"* Jan thought as she steeled herself for the moment when he would reach out to tear her to pieces.

Then an unexpectedly wonderful thing happened. When the beast was nearly upon her, he gently sank to its knees in the water and even though he continued to speak and to cry and although she could neither follow the language nor read his gestures, she suddenly knew that this creature meant her no harm. He too was here for a purpose.

Jan nearly swooned with relief.

"Oh, my God!" she thought, *"There can be no other explanation. Яω must have sent this beast to help me. This creature inhabits the planet within the spectrum of light for which the computer had reconfigured the ship just before it crashed. There can be no other reason for him to be here other than to assist me."*

With renewed confidence, Jan backed slowly toward Ma, until she was standing next to the body of her junior officer. She motioned for the monster to come closer. If he turned out to be hostile, at least she had a chance on dry land, she thought. But her emotions turned upside down once more when the gigantic body rose and began lurching through the water toward her. The nearer he came, the more fearsome he became, until Jan felt herself withering before him in terror once more.

Somehow, the monster felt, or understood, her alarm and he held the palms of his hands out in supplication. Jan acted immediately, motioning for him to pick up the Sub So and follow her.

Together, they climbed slowly back toward the To.

CHAPTER NINE

SEPTEMBER 3, 2002
FOLLOWING THE WOMAN FROM THE POND

Marvin was awakened with a start.

Something had crashed into the forest, very close to where he was hiding. It could only have been an airplane, he thought. Confused, he had no idea from which direction the noise of the disaster had come, but he was sure he would be engulfed by debris and hunkered down. As he looked out from his place of hiding, he could see chunks of debris flying in every direction from behind a knoll above him. Some of it landed in the pond. And then the forest was quiet: Deathly quiet.

A small heard of deer had been drinking at the pond. They pointed white tufted ears and licked their black noses, blinked long eyelashes and flexed their muscular thighs. They spiked their pointed tails and bounded away.

"Damn," Marvin said. He could hear their heavy hooves thump-thumping away in the soft mountain grass. A sharp hoof cracked a downed log. A jay scolded. At last the forest was completely quiet, except for a low wail that came from the lips of a woman who had stumbled and slid her way down the hill from the crash and staggered into the pond.

Marvin was scarcely able to breathe. Should he do something, he wondered? What could he do? Should he rush down and help the woman and tell her everything would be all right? Was everything all right? What would he be able to do to help her if she had been injured? Could someone she loved have perished in the crash? Should he scramble up the hill to see if there were survivors?

Unanswered questions poured through his mind.

Marvin had not moved when another woman emerged from the trees. He bolted forward with a start at what she seemed prepared to do.

It seemed that the second woman intended to shoot the first but the two began to talk and Marvin relaxed. But when the second woman pointed her weapon once more, Marvin knew he must act.

But what could he do, he was too far away? His rifle, he thought. Just firing the noisy weapon might prevent the second woman from shooting at all. At least she would know someone was watching. He would fire a shot to frighten her. But she looked awfully serious. No, he thought. That wouldn't be enough. She might shoot anyway.

"I could wing her," Marvin said with conviction.

He aimed his rifle at the second woman's shoulder, checking to see if the rifle's safety had been released. He pushed all of the air from his lungs, took in a huge breath and held it, wrapped his finger around the trigger, and waited, hoping the woman would change her mind. When it became obvious she would not, Marvin, resigned, aimed at her shoulder. He closed his eyes and fired, counting cities through the entire alphabet, dreading to look up. The woman was flat on her back in the mountain grass when he finally did. She wasn't moving. *"You've killed her,"* Marvin thought.

"My God," he cried, "I didn't want to kill nobody."

Marvin began to count cities out loud as he very carefully

climbed from his hiding place. When he had reached the ground, the rifle clattered down from the tree where he had left it, landing at his feet. He recoiled from the awful thing. First, he picked it up. Then, he threw it down. Picking it up a second time, he turned and started out into the pond with the weapon lying across his outstretched palms. He would give it to the woman. Surely she would see that he had not wanted to kill anyone. He counted cities aloud, as rapidly as possible, willing himself not to have a seizure.

At some point, the woman turned. A look of pure horror spread across her face as she acknowledged his presence. She winced away. Marvin could see fear replacing the mask of shock that, until now, had dominated her face. Deep inside, he knew she must be afraid of what he might do to her. Yet he could not prevent himself from moving forward. He stopped counting and began to beg for her forgiveness. Somehow, if he could only convince this woman that he had acted in her behalf, she would understand that he could not hurt her.

"Honest," he begged, still holding his rifle with both hands, "I only wanted to kill a deer. I only wanted to feed my family. She looked like she wanted to kill you. I only wanted to stop her, honest. Honest!"

The woman flung her hand at the rifle, knocking it aside.

That was when Marvin realized how beautiful she was.

Especially beautiful women had always cringed from his grotesque appearance. Marvin desperately wanted to get past that. He wanted to make her believe his good intentions. "Please try to understand," he implored, "I thought she was trying to kill you. Try to understand."

It was only when Marvin got down on his knees that the woman's expression began to relax. He could see her attitude change. Her face suddenly began to glow with elation as she retreated to the side of her attacker. It was with a profound sense of relief that Marvin responded to her gesture for help. "Now," he thought, "she will believe me." He began to explain again as he lunged from the cold water.

But the woman became frightened again. Perhaps it was his voice.

Marvin stopped begging.

He held out his hands in an attempt to demonstrate submission.

The woman finally seemed to tolerate his presence. She indicated for him to pick up the dead woman and he obliged. The woman was a feather in his arms.

"So small..." Marvin thought, *"...so beautiful."*

Never in his life had Marvin been so close to such extraordinarily beautiful women. Both were exceptionally fair, almost white, each with shockingly red hair and indescribable eyes: They could have been twins except for the fact that one was much larger than the other. Strangely, both women seemed to have no muscle tone, yet the one in his arms felt quite sturdy. She wore clothing that could pass for skin.

"She's almost naked," he thought, blushing. Marvin refused to look at her, sparing the dead woman any further embarrassment.

When the three reached the crest of the small hill, Marvin was shocked to find that a ship had crashed, yet remained intact in spite of the violence of the impact and not in pieces, as he had imagined. A huge furrow had been dug into the forest, ending in a log jam of trees, impaled by the body of the craft. Everything was smoking or steaming or hissing.

The triangular body of the ship was embedded into the mountain, yet appeared to be unharmed. The very size of the craft was unnerving, unbelievable in fact: It could easily have covered a football field. It glowed and yet it did not. Its surface shimmered beneath his feet and yet was solid, as Marvin and the woman walked up onto a nacelle toward a rectangular entry that was almost too narrow for Marvin and the woman he carried.

"This ain't no airplane," Marvin marveled, as he stepped through the hatch.

On entering the pocket cruiser, a third woman stood in his path. Menacingly, she drew and pointed her weapon at him, barring his way. Marvin knew instinctively that she would kill him if not for the woman from the pond. The two of them argued briefly. At last the woman put her weapon aside and turned. Together, the two of women walked ahead of the "brute" who carried their companion, through a series of long companionways, into the heart of the ship.

Marvin could not believe the things he saw.

Tiny gray creatures with large black eyes and very long arms filled every companionway: repairing, scurrying, moving things. Occasionally, one carried the body of a crew member. Those carrying bodies followed Marvin until a line formed behind him. They passed women with red hair, but just as often, orange, or even yellow.

Each person expressed shock (or disbelief) at his presence until she realized he was with the woman from the pond. They stepped aside obediently, but he could see distrust on their faces.

All spoke in a language he could not understand.

Often, their conversations seemed to occur inside his head.

Finally, the woman from the pond turned into a compartment, motioning for him to follow. She indicated a place where the woman he carried was to be placed and stepped aside. Many dead women were lying on adjacent metal tables. The gray creatures came in and deposited bodies without acknowledging him.

A voice, in a very clipped manner, sounding mechanical, filled the room from a source he could not pinpoint. Its message did not sound particularly urgent but the two women began an animated conversation, resulting in their abrupt departure from the compartment. In that moment, both had forgotten Marvin. For some time he stood next to the woman he had carried from the pond. Eventually, he began to look around. Never had he been in the presence of so many dead people.

They made him nervous and he began to count cities, at first under his breath and then aloud as he grew more and more anxious. “Don’t leave me here,” he suddenly cried.

Marvin began to search for a way out but the door through which he had entered was sealed and he grew agitated, pacing. He moved away from the dead woman from the pond.

Without warning, lights in the room began flashing, Marvin vented his frustration by screaming and pounding on the sealed door. He was terrified. The fact that he had never experienced this emotion was, in itself, overwhelming. His skin grew clammy and he felt the flush which precedes a seizure. Counting cities no longer helped. He searched for a niche which would allow him to hide until the event passed. He lifted a heavy cover of a shallow machine that looked like a refrigerator lying on its back, and looked inside. Inside, he found something that looked like a bed in the bottom. A small light glowed invitingly from within and he crawled inside without thinking, pulling the lid down until it clicked.

Even then he did not feel safe.

With the locking device secured, the mechanism into which Marvin had crawled began powering up automatically. A series of alternating lights flashed on the control panel above him indicated the system had initialized a standard operating cycle. Contact with the ship’s central computer was established electronically and pre-set sequencing codes activated a series of interval commands.

A central server was accessed and the machine began to function.

Without warning, the panel lights went out. A solid light came on a second later, indicating that an alternate series of codes had been activated. In less than one second, an emergency string of commands was initialized and the ship's computer began to grind its way into a search for a nearly infinite solution.

If an operator had been in attendance at that moment, the machine could have been sequenced down manually. Given no such intervention, functional control was rerouted, via a standard loop command, to the ship's main computer. Simultaneously, the ship's historical, technical, scientific and medical databases were accessed.

In a nanosecond, an enormous amount of power began to be diverted from the ship's power grid to handle an overload created by the inability of the ship's computer to function within pre-established parameters.

A warning light in OpCom came on. It went unnoticed.

The small light inside Marvin's container went out.

"Albuquerque," he screamed, "Boston, Cincinnati, Dover..."

Face down in the machine, Marvin slid into an epileptic seizure.

CHAPTER TEN

SEPTEMBER 3, 2002
THE DRONE INTERFACE

"The pocket cruiser To has been isolated, Master," Josh, said.

"Good."

Twenty-one years old and nearly at the end of his life cycle, Josh was a typical ál Ebon drone-interface. Once his superior intellect had been established at birth, he had been sold into service by parents who were happy not to have to support another mouth. The money from the sale of their son also provided temporary relief from a life of debt that plagued all citizens of ál Ebon.

From infancy, Josh's mind had been directed to mastering the sciences.

He had been integrated with his machine at eighteen.

At the moment, his task was to direct a battalion of robotic drones in the destruction of Ranjoshiteé. Twenty yards away, in every direction, others like himself oversaw similar battalions of drones in every part of the world and out into the space surrounding it and, in recent years, on other planets or moons.

To his left, a drone-interface oversaw the attack on the battle cruiser, Ja. On this floor alone, under an enormous, hermetically controlled, windowless, domed building, one thousand and sixty drone-interface guides operated simultaneously. Beyond that, on scores of tiers above and below Josh, more thousands of computer (or drone-interface) guides managed every other aspect of ǻl Ebon life.

Highly intelligent and rabidly focused, Josh was the eldest of these specialists. He, like the others, was nearly a machine: Yet the structure housing dozens of electronic components remained human. His entire adult existence had been spent at the command and control nexus of the ǻl Ebon fleet. A lifeless body, he whirred continually through the twenty square-meter workstation that was his home, oblivious to all of the people who surrounded him.

Like Josh, when a human "interface candidate" reached adult height, his or her back was severed below the ribs and the torso attached to a motorized cart, operated by a servo implanted in the brain. Each cranium was then welded to a headset into which a dozen chips were plugged, monitoring streams of linear data from the onboard computers of every asset within an assigned drone battalion.

Everyone was immediately fully operational. From this point in their lives, none were expected to live more than three years.

No guide experienced the sensation of time.

Strangely, only the larynx of an interface remained unimpaired. For, while each received commands via a direct electronic link to ǻl Ebon through the headset, he or she could only express outward communication to the Supreme Being audibly. Within the complex, the combined voices of the interface population, communicating tens of thousands of simultaneous outgoing communications to the Supreme Being, sounded like insane babble. Like the roar of a giant waterfall, it poured through the cavernous building unabated, day and night.

From the moment a person became a drone-interface, sleep requirements were satisfied by continuous automatic refreshment of the upper memory through the guide's hard drive. The drive regulated nourishment, flushed the system of waste and fulfilled any need for exercise or sexual pleasure that might be generated by the memory. Any physical requirement or enjoyment of this kind, of course, ran concurrently with the guide's work functions.

Josh's neatly trimmed fingernails, long since overgrown by the cuticles, lent his remaining persona a fragile, porcelain-like quality. His untoned arms, deeply veined hands and emaciated fingers were a blur of motion. They flew across the 360° keyboard surrounding him, the only movement of his body, as his chair scuttled endlessly through an oval workstation with blinding speed.

Josh was connected to the drone fleet in two ways. Four Isochips, buried deep in his brain, capable of calculating millions of kilobytes per second, received parallel streams of data from the onboard computers of each craft. His fingers sent outgoing commands through his enormous keyboard. A two-way conversation between Josh and any drone was not possible, yet he received and sent information, within his assigned data stream, to each drone singly or to every drone in his charge simultaneously.

Like all the others, Josh was in direct mental communication with ál Ebon, an unseen entity which seemed to envelop the space around him. As with every drone guide, ál Ebon commands filled his mind until it felt like the building itself was his master.

"The firing sequences of the To have been nullified, Master," he said.

"Good."

"It has flown into the atmosphere of the planet."

"Trapped," the Master mused.

"Shall I order other drones to follow?"

“All of them.”

“Including those engaging the Ja?”

“All of them.”

“Destroy the To, Master?”

“Destroy it.”

“The first squadrons have entered the atmosphere, Master.”

“Good.”

“The To seems to be in distress or…” Josh started.

“Distress?” ἁl Ebon interrupted.

“…out of control.”

“Explain.”

“The ship appears to have penetrated the atmosphere without plotting an entry solution.”

“Has it been crippled?” ἁl Ebon asked uncharacteristically.

“No, Master.”

“Where are the drones?” ἁl Ebon suddenly demanded.

“The cruiser seems to have crashed,” Josh said, ignoring his master’s last request.

“The drones, Josh.”

A moment passed. “Are you still in communication with Sub So Ma?” ἁl Ebon asked impatiently.

“I am receiving static, Master.”

“Explain.”

"She may be unconscious."

"Rouse her."

"Sub So Ma is awake," Josh said finally. "But not communicating."

"Stimulate her."

"Yes, Master."

"Ranjoshiteé has exited the ship unarmed, Master."

"Send Sub So Ma after her."

Again, several moments passed.

"She has confronted the So, Master."

"Kill her."

"She is dead, Master."

"Good."

"Not Ranjoshiteé, Master, Sub So Ma."

"Obliterate the To."

"The To cannot be located, Master."

"Preposterous."

CHAPTER ELEVEN

SEPTEMBER 3, 2002
THE FOUL SMELLING BEAST

As Jan and Dak, her personal guard, were returning to the bridge, Jan's mind was awash in a sea of extraordinary new considerations, provoked by the strange creature from the lake. She had flown above the surface of Atlantæ between the infra-red and ultra-violet spectrums of light many times. She had even skimmed close to the surface of the planet, but never had she seen any of the inhabitants. Nor had she expected to. Witnessing their smoke-covered cities through the eyes of the ship's computer had been enough.

Somehow, she had never accepted the idea that truly sentient, intelligent beings could occupy such a filthy environment. In addition, the Council had expressly forbidden pocket cruiser commanders or corsair pilots from landing on the surface while operating within this spectrum – even during an emergency.

Until now, the subject had been academic.

Now she had one of the primitive, foul-smelling beasts aboard her ship. Jan needed to remove it as quickly as possible.

Yet, if all of the inhabitants were as docile as the monster in the re-conformation lab seemed to be, she wondered, why hadn't the World Council explored the possibility of colonizing? After all, the cities above the ultra-violet spectrum of light occupied very different geographical locations on the planet. Many were on the ocean floor like Atlantae, most were buried under mountains.

If the council, for any reason, wanted to maintain a separation of the two civilizations, there seemed to be an overabundance of vehicles with which to accomplish this. The fact that both populations could neither see nor communicate with the other ought to represent an enormous barrier. But if colonization could give Atlantæ supremacy over the entire planet, perhaps an occupation could have a tangible, lasting value. After all, hadn't Roi Tan formed a coalition with other civilizations in the solar system in her desire to overcome the threat and the constant attacks on her fleet and civilians by the lifeless drones of ál Ebon?

Everyone and everything on the planet would be under the control of Atlantæ. Everything, that is, except the territory controlled by ál Ebon, wherever that was. Surprisingly, after over four hundred years, the council had never discovered the location of the madman and his culture of minions. As a result, every strategy, every tactic in this war had been reactive. Atlantae had never been able to control the fight. It could only defend but, given the recent victories of an entrenched, ever more powerful enemy, colonization of the middle world almost seemed prudent.

As they walked, Jan interrupted her musing to instruct Dak.

"Remove the ál Ebon implant from the Sub So," she said.

"Aye," Dak replied.

"Get her into ReCon first. I need her for the coming battle."

"Aye."

"And remove the beast from the ship."

"Immediately," Dak said with obvious disgust.

"Do not hurt it," Jan said authoritatively.

"And if it resists?"

"Under no circumstances are you to injure it. That thing prevented the Sub So from killing me. It carried her back, doing no harm to me. I can't prove it, but I'm sure it was sent to help me. In any event, I owe it an honor debt."

But the Uni Tau did not respond quickly enough for Jan.

"Understand?" she asked, looking to her guard for assurance.

"Yes, I understand. But it is the largest creature I have ever seen. How will we control it if it gets belligerent? We can't even communicate with it."

"Use a hypo if you have to."

"Aye."

"Computer," So Jan said, "how many of the crew were killed?"

"Twenty-four," the computer reported.

"And injured?"

"Ten."

"Only ten of us are functioning?"

"Four of the injured are at their stations," the computer reported.

"How long will it take to refresh the injured?"

"Two hours and twenty-one minutes," the computer responded.

"Begin immediately."

"All injured, report to ReCon One and Two," the computer announced ship-wide.

"And the re-conformation of the twenty-four dead?" So Jan asked.

"An additional eleven hours and forty seven minutes."

"Have the injured assist with the dead once they have been returned to duty."

"The chamber is jammed in ReCon One," the computer interrupted.

"Get back there, Dak," Jan ordered.

The Uni Tau ran back in the direction from which they had come.

The So continued on. "Computer," Jan said, "project the time the drone interfaces will need to calculate our location now that the To has been reconfigured to this spectrum."

"A minimum of six hours and thirty-one minutes," the computer responded one second later.

"What is the ship's operational situation?" she asked.

"There is a ninety three percent probability that all flight systems are…" the computer began, then discontinued its report.

"Computer, respond!" So Jan said.

The computer remained silent. The lights in the companionway began to dim, flickered and went out, just as Jan arrived at the entry hatch to the bridge. By feel, in pitch black, she inserted her identity card into the side of the senior officer's security-lock-keypad, punched in her clearance code and pushed the door open manually.

"Bridge guard, report," Jan said as she stepped onto the bridge.

"The main computer just went down," the guard said redundantly.

CHAPTER TWELVE

SEPTEMBER 3, 2002
CONFRONTING A THREAT

The power began to fail ship-wide just as Dak reached ReCon One. Sections of the ship sequentially and systematically plunged into impenetrable blackness. On entering the compartment, she heard muffled screams and a terrible thrashing sound that seemed to emanate from everywhere at once inside the lab. She was unable to identify a source.

"The beast has managed to corner or injure the lab tech," Dak thought and she slowly drew her weapon, inching her way into the interior of the compartment. She tripped after taking only a few steps and fell into one of the tables in the middle of the room. Dak went down, grasping for support, shoving her hand onto the body of a dead crewmate in the process. The person had not yet cooled, and was soft and pliable under her pressure. There was a tiny sucking sound as her hand came away, her fingers sticky and wet.

Dak shrank away from the table. Unnerved, she cried in anguish.

In two hundred sixty years as a crew member of the To, Dak had never experienced battle death, one of the great benefits of crewing under So Jan. In addition, the ReCon team members continually refreshed the crew, keeping everyone young, renewing bodies and minds, until aging and dying had become virtually unknown. Dak had been, for hundreds of years, a warrior of the mind, not of physical contact. She had never experienced hand to hand combat, nor had she killed. At this moment, Dak found herself unprepared for the emotions aroused by coming so intimately in contact with the dead and she retched violently.

An eternity seemed to pass before Dak began to grope once more.

The unrelenting totality of darkness was, in itself… terrifying, as was the fear of not knowing what she would find. Disorienting, the muffled screams echoing throughout the compartment were completely debilitating. To make matters worse, her hands were constantly in contact with the bodies of bloodied and dismembered shipmates and friends. Although she knew they would be rejuvenated in the ReCon chambers, the grizzly experience wore on her. About to give up, she stumbled, at last, upon the source of the thrashing noises by accident. Relief flooded through her body when she came to realize the noises had been coming from within one of the ReCon chambers.

“'The lab tech,” Dak mouthed silently. Wanting desperately to understand the source of her anxiety, she removed her weapon from its lock and flicked away the safety. Setting its weakest mode, she discharged the weapon, using the few seconds the narrow beam emanated as a light source.

“I hope you're safe,” she thought. She beamed the control panel, looking for any way to turn the chamber off.

“Oh, my God!” she whispered, sweeping light across her feet.

The machine was hard at work, blanketing the compartment floor with endless streams of latex printouts, and the process showed no sign of abating. She had not yet found a shut-off switch but the thrashing and the screaming slowly began to subside until the compartment was, at last, eerily quiet, except for the whoosh of the latex being pushed onto the floor, and the beating of Dak's heart as it pumped blood past her eardrums with the thud of a trip hammer.

She made an attempt to read the printouts but the mathematical calculations were gibberish to her.

Above the machine, electronic panel lights blinked on and off monotonously, clicking each time they went black. A small, battery-driven, solid-state monitor remained on, however, its light burning with an extremely low intensity. It indicated that the chamber was activated, and in the process of diverting every bit of the ship's available power to the ReCon station. But like a battery with a broken core, the chamber was sucking energy from the grid faster than the ship's generators could produce it. At this rate, the ship was not likely to take off, little alone make it to orbit and reenter the battle.

"We could be marooned," Dak moaned.

Behind her, the lab technician gasped.

"Where have you been," Dak demanded.

"Unconscious in the crew's compartment. And then I helped with the litters. What a mess!"

"Can you tell me what's happening here?" Dak said.

The technician probed with an efficient little pocket laser, searching for and finding the first of the printouts. She carefully read each line.

"Something very large is in the chamber," she said finally.

"What?"

"I don't know. But whatever is in there is really big. And it's dense, so dense that the chamber is having a hard time calculating a recon. In addition, the machine seems to have accessed every electronically stored record on the ship: astrometrics, physics, literature, everything. The chamber is trying to re-conform whatever this thing is but the computations are massive. It would be like trying to calculate infinity. The computer has practically ground to a stop and is simply inching along. At this rate, it will take hours for the machine to begin running normally again. In the meantime – it's sucking up all available power."

"Oh, my God!" Dak said quietly.

"What?" It was the technician's turn to utter the word.

"It's in there!"

"What?" the tech cried.

"What?" Jan echoed, as she entered the lab. She had come all the way across the ship using her weapon as a light source.

The technician began to explain once more but stumbled miserably and restarted. Dak interrupted impatiently. "The monster is in the damned machine and it can't handle the load. It is as if the computer is calculating infinity. While the ReCon chamber calculates infinity, the entire ship is providing power, but it's not enough."

"Turn it off," Jan ordered.

"I can't," the technician said.

"Unplug it."

"ReCon is an adjunct of the mainframe. The whole thing will have to be dismantled."

"How long will that take?"

"In dry dock: A week. Out here: who knows."

"You have six hours," Jan said. "ǿl Ebon will be all over us after that."

CHAPTER THIRTEEN

SEPTEMBER 3, 2002
TRAPPED

After seven hours of total darkness, the central computer had become marginally functional. The ship's interior lights slowly began working, although at an extremely low intensity. Occasionally, they flickered, threatening to go out once more. All of the ship's major functions: life support, engineering, fire control, etc., remained down.

The air grew stale and outside hatches had been opened to let in fresh air. The Aegis was the only critical function of the ship which remained operational, because it was powered by a separate source of energy, controlled by a secondary computer. In case the Aegis' auxiliary computer ever went down, say in battle, as a result of a direct hit, for example, its function could be manually switched to the main computer. That had never happened.

The To was eerily quiet.

Outside the ship, the sun began setting into the western horizon, blood red and brooding. Voluminous black clouds drifted ominously across its face, driven by a large storm in the Gulf of Mexico. Cold autumn winds whipped dust from the outside world through the ship's interior companionways. Always immaculate, the "Pride of the Fleet" felt like an abandoned shack to crewmen who had spent their lives keeping the ship in top condition.

Marvin's small herd of deer ate dainty shoots from a forest floor which had been disturbed by the crash of the stricken craft. A small bear drank quietly from the rancher's pond.

Of the crew members remaining at their work, a guard stood close to Jan for much of the time, her weapon unlocked. The lab tech and Dak hovered nervously inside the lab, monitoring the chamber. Although wounded, a medic, third class, did what she could to assist the injured. Another of the wounded continually monitored the central computer for any sign of mitigation, manning a hand held communications transmitter directly linked to the So. A cook did what she could to make nourishment available for those who would eat. The remaining crew members stood on the starboard nacelle, marveling at a sunset much different, in this spectrum, than their own.

Jan remained on the bridge, returning to the ReCon lab every hour or so to get a first-hand report on the status of the chamber. Between visits, her guard acted as a runner, carrying any informational updates, which remained consistently unchanged throughout the day. Outwardly, as always, So Jan remained calm. Inside, her mind reflected the turmoil expressed by Dak and the lab tech who milled about ReCon One continuously, like caged rats.

Jan brooded in her battle command seat. "If we don't get off the surface, we're going to get scorched," Jan muttered to herself. "Computer," she said, "how long until an ál Ebon interface calculates this position?"

"The computer can no longer estimate this eventuality," the computer reported lazily, dragging the words as if its synthesized voice were being squeezed through a milling press.

"Explain."

"The projected computation time has elapsed."

"When can we expect an attack?"

"Any time after nineteen hundred thirty hours."

"That was an hour ago."

Exasperated, Jan stalked off the bridge, heading for ReCon One with her guard in tow.

"This ship is filthy," she said as she entered the lab.

"Aye," the guard responded self-consciously.

The panel above the ReCon chamber came to life as Jan moved into the compartment. The chamber lid popped open.

"Thank goodness," the lab tech said.

"Draw your weapons," Jan commanded both Uni Taus.

Without warning, the ship's lights returned to full strength, temporarily blinding everyone in the compartment.

"...obot fighters have located the To," the computer reported, coming out of its sleep.

"Lift the lid," Jan said to the tech, indicating the chamber. "Steady," she cautioned.

"The ship will be under attack in one minute and thirty-four seconds," the computer reported.

"We have to do something," Dak said with a frantic edge in her voice.

The other bridge guard rebuked her with a nudge.

"We could all be killed!" Dak cried.

"Remain calm," Jan said.

The lab tech lifted the lid and looked into the chamber with arms extended across the opening.

"Oh, my God!" she whispered.

"What?" Dak cried hysterically.

"Remain calm," Jan repeated.

Simultaneously, and without warning, a deep voice resonated from inside the chamber. "Computer, plot a reconfiguration solution that conforms with the spectrum of light below infrared."

The tech winced and, as one, Jan and her guards stepped back.

"The computer cannot respond to this command. The computer does not recognize the voice print," the computer reported.

At that moment, the ál Ebon drone nearest to the To fired, scoring a direct hit, which bounced harmlessly off the protective Aegis.

Inside the ship, however, the blast felt horrific as the impact had not been absorbed by the planet's surface. Instead, it had been reflected back into the ship, doubling the impact.

"Computer," Jan immediately commanded, "Plot a spectral reconfiguration solution..." She was interrupted by a second direct hit as it smashed against the Aegis.

"The Aegis will be penetrated in twenty-six seconds," the computer reported.

"...to conform with the spectrum of light below infrared." Jan shouted.

"Spectral reconfiguration solution plotted," the computer reported one second later.

"Computer, alter the ship's spectral configuration."

The ambient light changed slightly from azure to pink as a third missile crashed into the To. The ship's hull rang sharply under the impact, reverberating cruelly into her earthly berth.

"The Aegis has been penetrated," The computer reported.

"Computer, give me an operational status report," So Jan said.

"There is a one hundred percent probability that a severe hull breach has occurred in fire control, aft," The computer reported as if the entire ship's complement had been at their stations. "There is ninety seven percent probability," the computer continued, "that everyone in the aft fire control station has been killed. There is a…"

The computer stopped reporting as a fourth explosion raged directly against the hull of the ship.

Mercifully, the To was not fired upon again.

Everything went black once more.

CHAPTER FOURTEEN

SEPTEMBER 3, 2002
SOMEWHERE IN THE GOBI DESERT

"The To has been destroyed, Master," Josh reported.

"No," ál Ebon replied thoughtfully.

"Yes, Master, the cruiser took four direct hits. It was completely obliterated. No trace of the craft remains."

"It does not feel like the To has been destroyed," ál Ebon said quietly. "Continue to scan the area."

A long silence ensued.

"Two hundred and forty scans have been made of the entire area," Josh said at last. "There is no sign of the To."

ál Ebon did not respond.

"Master?"

"Scan the ultra-high frequencies," ál Ebon said.

"Yes, master."

ál Ebon grew impatient. "Well?" he demanded.

"Nothing."

"And the Ja?"

"The Ja will enter Penumbra's space in eleven hours and twenty three minutes, Master."

"Intercept and destroy the Ja."

"This is not possible, Master."

"Explain."

"With all drones moving in unison, drone-interface specialists will not be able to coordi…"

"Nonsense."

"Command and control is the problem," Josh said.

"Why has this become an issue now?"

"Until now, drone-interface has been limited to squadrons, never has the entire fleet needed to act in unison."

"And?"

"It is a matter of programming, Master."

"The answer is simple, Josh."

"Master?"

"Re-program everything."

Josh did not respond.

"What are you doing, Josh?"

"Writing new code, Master."

"How long will this take?"

Josh did not respond.

"Josh?"

"One moment, Master."

"Josh?"

"Twenty three hours, thirty seven minutes and fifteen seconds, Master."

ál Ebon did not respond.

"Master?"

"How long to download the software and regiment the required force to attack Penumbra?"

"One hour and fourteen minutes," Josh said.

"How long will it take the drones to reach Penumbra?"

"Twenty-eight hours, twelve minutes and th…"

"Send them."

"Yes, Master."

"How long will it take for this issue to become critical?"

"One day, Master."

"That is how long you have to re-write the code, Josh."

"Are the drones expendable?"

"Yes."

"Then your command is possible."

"You are getting old, Josh."

"Master?"

"When our work has been completed, Josh, disconnect yourself from your station and you will be assisted as you exit the facility."

"I will die?'

"Yes, Josh, you will die."

Josh's hands and arms flew across the keyboards, writing code and relaying a new series of commands. For the remainder of the afternoon, Josh monitored incoming linear digital data from the squadrons as they amassed, orbiting the planet like swarms of fire ants, readying to cross. He assessed strengths. He evaluated weaknesses. There were none. After two days of unremitting battle, his forces had emerged nearly undamaged. Except for casualties inflicted by the To, the ál Ebon fleet had escaped practically unscathed. He transmitted coordinates for the last known area of near space in which the Ja had been recorded, sending scouts.

"The battle cruiser has moved closer," Josh reported.

"Toward Penumbra," ál Ebon said. "Attack Penumbra as well," he commanded.

"The Ja will be entering lunar space in four hours and fifty-six minutes," Josh reported moments later. "The launch of the drones toward Penumbra will commence in eighteen hours and twenty-four minutes, Master," he said.

"Leave a squadron behind," ál Ebon commanded. "Continue to scan for the To."

"Three damaged attack cruisers remain in orbit, Master."

"Eliminate them."

"They are well out of the flight path to Penumbra, Master."

"Explain."

"They are on the opposite side of the planet from the embarkation point."

"How long to destroy the three remaining puny USNA cruisers and return to the assembly area?"

"One hour and three minutes."

"Too long. Attack Penumbra."

"Yes, Master."

"Good," ál Ebon said, "They will all be there."

"Master?"

"All of my enemies."

"On Penumbra, Master?"

"This will be a glorious day," ál Ebon exulted. "First, the elimination of Ranjoshiteé, and now, Roi Tan and her squalid abettors and minions. Alone, they do not have the power to attack me and together, these unholy satraps and filthy despots cannot stop my drone legions from attacking them. In the end, I will purge Indus of their blasphemous babble about freedom and end the contemptible consumption of my wealth. Soon, I will cleanse the solar system. The entire solar system will be ál Ebon. Soon, indeed. Where once I sought only to bring Indus to a state of enlightened fellowship, I now stand on the verge of illuminating all. What a glorious day. Soon ál Ebon will rule the universe itself."

"ál Ebon!" Josh shouted.

"A glorious day," ál Ebon whispered.

"ál Ebon!" Josh shouted.

"ál Ebon!" every drone interface shouted in unison.

CHAPTER FIFTEEN

SEPTEMBER 3, 2002
THE AWAKENING

"I am Marvin," the naked man said to the Commander of the To. A unanimous gasp issued from the warrior women huddled before him. Bunched together, they could only watch as he lifted himself from the chamber and, as one, they retreated farther into the compartment.

"Who are you?" he asked the nearest person to him.

So Jan winced. She stood in front of her two guards. Each held a weapon at the ready, both looked as though they might faint and all three were riding rubbery legs. A fourth woman stood behind everyone, looking as though she would flee at the slightest provocation. Strangely, she was the most curious but fear overrode caution, and she pushed off the back of the closest guard with her fingertips, seeking room between herself and any possibility of disaster. All of the women, except for So Jan, stood less than five feet tall. The Commander was a giant compared to her crew.

Jan was the first to speak. "Mar," she repeated softly.

Marvin worked to understand. It was as though she were trying to begin a conversation using the simplest syllable in order to pronounce his entire name correctly. Or was it her name, instead? He could not tell. The two of them nodded their heads in apparent agreement, but enormous disbelief was written across the faces of both.

So Jan was giddy from everything she had just witnessed.

A beast had entered the ReCon chamber, but was no longer there. Instead, a huge unclothed being had emerged from the chamber in its place, a massive, beautiful being, unlike anything she had ever seen. Where the monster had been filthy and foul of stench, this one smelled of calloberry in autumn.

A few of the prominent features of the original creature remained in the broad nose and wide forehead, but his face had been re-sculpted in the image of an Atlantæn. He was soft skinned and his breath was sweet and he had no facial hair. Only a thin measure of silk-like strands rose from atop his wide head. Sleek and refined, his hair could have been plucked from the virgin underbelly of a newborn swan. And although he barely stood a few inches above So Jan, he was wide. Three of her crew members would be able to stand side by side in the shadow of his back.

Stunned to a state of numbness by the changes made to this man, Jan had neither recognized that this magnificent creature was now speaking in her language, perfectly, or that he had correctly used the idiom of the warrior class.

"What does Mar mean?" she asked tentatively.

"Not Mar… Marvin."

"Mar Vin," she repeated carefully.

A thought awakened in her memory. "The Tsosa will come into being today," Ma had said. *"Oh, my God!"* Jan thought, *"this creature wasn't brought here to save me at all. I was brought to this place to find him,"* and in that one brief second, her life finally had meaning.

She had started the day in battle and while under attack, commanded her ship into the atmosphere of the planet without directing the shields; no trajectory had been plotted; nor had there been pitch control, guidance or landing solutions. The ship had crashed onto its surface. She had survived an attempt on her life, and was saved from death by this entity in his previous form. And last but certainly not least, his quick thinking had, only moments earlier, saved her entire ship from certain annihilation with his rapid analysis and astute advice, a second rescue by him within a matter of hours.

Who else could he be?

"Is Mar another word for Tsosa?" she asked breathlessly.

"The Tsosa," the lab tech repeated with certainty.

"Call me Marvin," the entity said with a twinkle in his eye, shaking his head positively but ignoring her question.

"Mar Vin," Jan tried again.

"Are there any clothes on this ship that I might be able to wear?"Marvin asked, looking from one guard to another.

"I, I don't know," Jan responded, also looking hopefully at her guards.

No one had ever seen a creature this large and in answer, they shriveled away from her.

"What do they call you?" the man asked, looking squarely into the eyes of the So.

"So Jan," the lab tech blurted. "She is So Jan."

"So Jan," Marvin said quietly, "You are the one I have come here to see."

"The Tsosa!" Jan breathed, dropping onto both knees.

Sub Tau Dak raised her weapon an inch, but the other guard got down as well, her face reflecting surprise and awe instead of fear.

"I am not the Tsosa." Marvin said patiently.

"But how can I know you are not the Tsosa," Jan implored.

"Believe me, I am not."

"I don't believe you," she cried.

Marvin smiled.

"Except for Яω, you are the most powerful being I have ever seen."

"All living beings have it within themselves to be a Tsosa," Marvin said quietly, offering his hand to Jan. "Please get up," he said. "We need to act."

Galvanized into action, Jan rose without taking the offered hand.

"What must we do?" she asked.

"Get this ship off the ground," the naked man said. "And find me some clothes."

Jan looked at him for the first time. "Oh, my God!" she said.

CHAPTER SIXTEEN

SEPTEMBER 3, 2002
PENUMBRA

While the drone armies gathered at the outer edge of the atmosphere, en masse, to cross the void between the world called Indus and its only moon, the Ja entered Penumbra's space. The largest ship in the solar system, it belied its power and speed by appearing to labor slowly into the assigned berth of honor, directly above the city.

The arrival was indeed a show. Hundreds of corsairs escorted the mile-wide battle cruiser with its nine accompanying pocket cruisers. The armada flowed into the pristine space above the city looking, beautifully, like a swarm of fireflies announcing a massive, floating, summer carnival.

Until now, except for the Martian fleet, only single caravels or small groups of ships had arrived from moons and worlds across the solar system. Each respectfully requested and was granted a berth above the colony. For days and weeks, their running lights were dark in the night sky like a growing number of holes against the Milky Way.

Their crews descended in small, well-mannered groups for quiet liberty, and commanding officers called on the constabulary and the offices of the governor as a formality.

Now the Ja flooded the space around Penumbra with spectacular, pulsating beams of light in every color imaginable. The air-lock canopy surrounding the colony was awash in the glow of the giant cruiser's presence. Brightly lit corsairs flew close to the city's nearly invisible protective covering and across the bow of every ship in the sky.

Soon the Ionian representative joined the revelry, and the tiny frigate from Titan responded as well. Eventually, even the conservative Martian contingent entered into the display with joyous participation. Within the hour, all of the envoys from every part of the civilized solar system had proudly announced their partnership in the conference.

Beneath the hundreds of craft filling its skies, lights from the colony were cheerful. Festively, the Penumbrians, under the massive canopy protecting them from the void, cheered. There had never been such a celebration and everyone was caught up in the moment.

Penumbra, as a protectorate of Atlantæ, could not be a signer in the newly formed Union of Solar States but its inhabitants were supportive, if somewhat tentative. Until now they had been free of the devastating attacks that plagued the rest of the solar system. As happy as they might be in the moment, they wanted desperately to avoid coming under the gun sights of the ɑ́l Ebon robot drones. The colony, in spite of its five hundred-year existence, was still an outpost, a jumping off point between Atlantæ and its trading partners around the solar system, and wanted no part of the ancient war.

As such, its citizens considered Penumbra neutral even if their leaders did not. Occasionally, the governor perfunctorily petitioned for independent status to remind his constituents of his loyalty to their cause, and to reawaken the World Council of Penumbra's importance to the greater trading community. As a result of his gamesmanship, Penumbrians were wealthy, educated and highly respected by the members of Atlantae's governing body – and one of the principal reasons Roi Tan had chosen this site for the signing of the charter.

Roi Tan and Sub Roi Bon stood in PriOps, enjoying the excitement.

"This moment feels good," Tan said.

"Uneventful is good," Bon mused.

"Yes."

"Communications is back on line."

"Good," Tan said. "Any news of the ships we left behind?"

"Three have returned to the surface for repairs. Te and Jap made it under power, but Corju had to be towed. Seven more are limping to Penumbra behind us, scheduled to arrive in about three hours. The Seventh Fleet has been reduced to nine pocket cruisers and four hundred twenty corsairs. One day later, the Fifth Fleet was also involved in a protracted battle, suffering similar losses until…"

"Until?"

"The ál Ebon drones inexplicably quit the battle."

"And the To?"

"Lost."

"Um."

"It's a shame."

"The remaining cruisers?"

"So Mano of the Set has set up a watch on the perimeter of the stratosphere with the nine remaining cruisers from the Seventh and three from the Fifth."

Roi Tan said nothing.

"ál Ebon drones have been massing," the Sub Roi said.

"To what purpose?"

"What else?"

"The conference," Tan said resolutely.

"When is the signing supposed to take place?"

"Sixteen hundred, tomorrow afternoon."

"If the drones leave orbit now, with their speed, they will arrive before the conference ends."

"I'll cut everything short. We'll be gone."

"They'll catch us going back."

"Maybe," Tan said quietly.

The Sub Roi looked at her skeptically.

"I have a plan," Tan said finally.

"Want to fill me in?"

"It's too early."

"A suicide mission," Bon uttered unerringly, after a moment had elapsed. She was immediately at peace with the idea. Her calmness in the face of annihilation was a surprise to Tan, who remained silent, enjoying the festivities.

"I thought so," the Sub Roi said under her breath after a while.

Tan looked at her Fleet Admiral out of the corner of her eye as if to say, “What makes you so damned smart?”

“When were you going to tell me,” the Sub Roi whispered, not wanting to arouse the interest of the Commander of the ship, who had moved within hearing range. After a moment, the So walked to the other side of the flying bridge. When they were alone once more, Tan resumed the conversation.

“I might not have,” she said quietly.

“I see.”

“We can set ál Ebon back three hundred years. It will give the Union time to survive. And the Union can win this war with enough time. But with Atlantæ’s current technology, we no longer offer any competition to the drones. Our ships are too big – too fat. Corsairs can match the speed, but not the range. Pocket cruisers have the edge on tactics and firepower, but no legs. The Martians will never have the technology and the Ionians do, but are not fearless like our corsair pilots and pocket cruiser commanders. One of the great benefits of this pact is that we will be able to bring many important elements together at last, including Ionian technology and our pilots.

“Do you know the most frightening thing of all? The newest drone has the capability of breaking into separate fighting units once it’s on the ground: A perfect invading force. Yes. Without the treaty, the strategy and tactics of this war would soon change and in the very near future, drones will be walking through our streets.”

Tan paused for effect.

“But ál Ebon,” she continued, “has one glaring weakness, and for him, it’s a back breaker: the inability to produce drones quickly. So. We’ll let them surround us and – WHAM – we take away their power to make war. ”

Despite the intensity of their conversation, the Supreme

Commander and the Fleet Admiral looked to the crew on the bridge as though they were enjoying the show and the entire bridge crew was content as they went about their work.

"We must hit them hard," Tan said. "Now!"

She drove a fist hard into the other hand.

The So turned with a puzzled look and went back to her business.

"We may never get an opportunity like this again," Tan said.

"Where did you get this idea?" the Sub Roi asked.

"It is So Jan's"

"How long have you kept this to yourself."

"A year. No… More."

"And you were waiting for…?"

"The conference."

"Oh, my God!" the Sub Roi said to herself. "The perfect moment."

"Yes."

"ál Ebon will think we're cornered. He'll know the leaders of the system have come together and throw everything at us."

"Yes."

"How does So Jan fit into the plan, if you don't mind telling me."

"The To carries a second bomb. A back-up, so-to-speak."

"Carried," the Sub Roi corrected.

"Yes," Tan said sadly. "It's too bad she'll miss this fight."

"Yes," the Sub Roi echoed. "What's the mechanism?"

"The bomb?"

"Yes, what is it?"

"A Cobalt."

Finally, the Sub Roi looked shocked. "What about Penumbra?" she asked. "We'll destroy them. They don't deserve that."

"I want to be on the front side of the moon when we light off. If not, the loss of the colony is a small price to pay."

"And Atlantæ?"

"It depends on how close we are to the planet."

"Oh, my God!"

"The council knows. They approved the plan unanimously. But, like I said, it's a small price to pay… a small price, indeed."

"What about the Union ambassadors?"

"I'll tell them as the signing ceremony is ending. They'll get the hell out of here."

Tan continued to watch the light show with a small smile on her face.

The Sub Roi was silent for a long time.

"How?" she asked finally.

"The computer is rigged to detonate the device with a word from me."

CHAPTER SEVENTEEN

SEPTEMBER 4, 2002
CRISIS ON THE BRIDGE

When Marvin entered the bridge, Uni Tau Dak took immediate exception. Without So Jan on the bridge, she was in charge and her Battle Quarters mandate was to admit approved personnel only. She immediately acted by shoving Marvin in the chest with the butt of her hand, fingers curled around a laser weapon in an attempt to prevent his entry, but it was she who was forced to move as she could not budge him and was compelled to take a step backward to recover.

Recognizing that raw power would never work against a being of this size and strength, Dak brought her weapon to bear, pointing it into Marvin's face. Like a striking cobra, he grabbed her wrist and pushed the weapon above her head. Reflexively, she fired, the blast lighting the room like a strobe just as So Jan entered.

"I know men are not allowed on your ships, let alone the bridge of a cruiser," Marvin said emotionlessly into the side of Dak's face.

Telepathically, he continued. "I'm sorry I can't be an approved member of your crew for this mission. But… I can't. You are going to have to put up with me the way I am. And I need to be here."

Assessing the situation correctly, Jan spoke directly to Marvin.

"Leave the bridge," she ordered, motioning for a second Uni Tau to accompany him. "Wait outside with him, Pax," she commanded.

"Aye," Pax said.

"Did you learn anything?" Jan asked Dak when the compartment door had been secured behind them.

"I..."

"Give him free access to the ship."

"Against regu..."

"Yes."

"I will have to enter this into my log."

"Very well. In the meantime, I am going to ask him to come back."

Dak's face hardened.

Jan turned away. ""Computer," she asked, "what is the current operational situation?"

"The hull breech in fire control aft has been repaired," the computer reported. "All fire control stations are fully operational.

"The forward missile compartments have been repaired and are fully operational. Missile seven is secure in its berth. The hull has been scanned and small repairs will have been completed in seventeen locations on the outer hull, six on the interior. All Aegis systems are functioning norm..." the computer droned on.

Jan turned back to Dak. "Sheath your weapon," she commanded.

Dak complied.

The computer completed its report and fell silent.

"Grant him full access," Jan said, her voice echoing slightly in the silent compartment.

"Aye," Dak said.

"Computer, report on the status of Sub So Ma," Jan said.

"Sub So Ma will be returned to duty in one hour."

Jan ordered Dak a second time, to invite Mar Vin to return to the bridge.

"Aye."

"Computer, report on the status of the injured crew members."

"All have been returned to their stations," the computer reported.

"And those who were killed?"

Jan stared at Dak, who sullenly turned her head toward the entry hatch, but had not moved.

"Seven have been taken to sickbay and are recovering. Of the seventeen remaining, two are in ReCons 1 and 2. The remainder are in stasis."

Jan turned to Dak. "Now!" she commanded.

Dak hesitated at the hatch, finally pushing the release mechanism to reveal Marvin and Pax who were standing quietly, just outside. Oddly, it looked to Dak as though the two were communicating with each other, although neither was speaking. As one, they moved to reenter the bridge.

"Computer, when will the ship be fully operational?" Jan asked.

"An additional crew member is required in ComNav, three in Engineering, one in Astrometrics, one in…"

"Computer," So Jan interrupted, "Plot a lift-off solution."

"A lift-off solution has been plotted," the computer reported one second later.

"Uni Tau Dak, you are permanently assigned to Mar Vin as his personal guard."

"Aye."

"Launch."

"Belay that," Marvin ordered. Dak pulled her weapon once more and moved slightly away from Marvin. She looked incredibly small standing next to him and inordinately brave, but he had countermanded a lawful order by the So and this was not going to be allowed to stand.

"Back outside," Dak commanded.

"Computer, belay that," Jan said. The pocket cruiser settled softly back into its earthly cradle.

Jan pointed a finger at Dak. "I ordered you to be his personal guard, Dak. Now, do just that. Sheath your weapon.

Dak reluctantly backed away.

"What am I missing, Mar Vin?" Jan asked.

"The ship is currently in ál Ebon space, undetected, and you have stealth capabilities."

Dak held her weapon above its holster but did not sheath it, waiting.

Jan turned toward NavCom but did not speak, locked in thought.

"When in the ReCon chamber, I absorbed everything in your libraries, So Jan," Marvin said.

"So!" Dak shot.

"Yes?" Jan said.

"According to one of Atlantae's most preeminent historians, Roi Earn, in her paper titled Chaos is Borne, written in 1642, she describes ά́l Ebon as a culture unable, ever, to erect great cities," Marvin said.

"So!" Dak shot again.

"…but he has built one great complex, from which he has ruled unchallenged for centuries."

"Make sense!" Dak shouted.

"Something that large must be detectable."

"Aye," Jan said.

CHAPTER EIGHTEEN

SEPTEMBER 4, 2002
PENUMBRA IN PERIL

The new protocols had been written and drones of the mighty ál Ebon fleets gathered at the edge of space awaiting the input of final codes when, en masse, they would scurry to Penumbra to destroy Roi Tan and her squalid abettors and minions, eradicate the satraps and despots of the universe, and end this "mighty" but ill-advised coalition before it could become a reality. Information, research, raw materials, technological resources and experience would never be shared by the enemies of ál Ebon in an attempt to bring this war to an end. No, ál Ebon would end the war on his terms and in his own time, and the time was now.

"The Supreme Commander of the United Nations Space Command," ál Ebon scoffed, "now at the conference on Penumbra, will die; and the Union ambassadors and government leaders of the Universe who have enlisted in her folly against me, will die with her. It has taken so long," he mused.

In the hours before his final victory, with his greatest achievement finally within his grasp, ál Ebon instructed the thousands of drone-interface specialists to power down their communications systems. From this moment on, interaction with the entire armada would be routed through Josh alone in order to insure absolute control as ál Ebon began his final assault on Roi Tan.

With ál Ebon communications transmitted only through Josh, the entire center fell eerily silent. Every drone-interface would be allowed to participate in this glorious victory, but only by listening. The only commands to which the fleets would respond would come from ál Ebon alone.

"One squadron is still searching for the To, Master."

"State its progress."

"A search of the ultra violet spectrum has been completed, Master."

"The entire spectrum?"

"One thousand hectares around the crash site, Master."

"And now?"

"It is about to search the same area between ultra violet and infra red."

"Continue scanning the ultra violet spectrum, Josh."

Josh did not respond.

"Josh?"

"Master?"

A long silence ensued.

"Ordering half the squadron to continue searching, ordering half the squa…" Josh started.

"Very good, Josh."

“Master?”

“Yes?”

“Will dying be painful?”

CHAPTER NINETEEN

SEPTEMBER 4, 2002
MA STARTS A WAR WITH THE MAR VIN

Dak was alone on the bridge when Ma was returned to duty.

"Where is So Jan?" Ma barked through her teeth.

"With the buffoon."

"The buffoon?"

"The Mar Vin."

"You don't sound so happy, Dak."

"Oh?"

"Is something bothering you, Uni Tau?"

"I have been assigned to guard the Mar Vin."

"The Mar Vin?"

"The one who killed you."

"Oh?"

"So Jan believes he is the Tsosa."

Ma was surprised and it showed.

"So Jan must trust you," Ma said guardedly after a moment.

"Punishment."

"For?"

"Everything! He orders So Jan around and I can't stand it. He blocked the ReCon chamber for over a day, making it impossible to reconstitute any of the crew in a timely way. He does not have clearance to enter any secure station and when I tried to block his entry to the bridge, I was countermanded. He was welcomed eagerly by the So. And then there's the fact that he's a man and men are never stationed aboard a warship for an uncountable number of reasons. They are never given access to anything, especially not the bridge of a battle cruiser. And finally, he has a big ass."

"I wondered who it might be," Ma mused.

"What?"

"The Tsosa."

"Everyone thinks the Tsosa is a myth in spite of everything that has happened," Dak said.

"Everyone?"

Dak stared in disbelief. She found it impossible to answer a question she deemed ridiculous.

"Not a myth," Ma said, shaking her head.

"No?"

"He was to come yesterday, and here he is."

"What?"

"He is here."

"You're as nuts as she is."

"He must be neutralized," Ma said quietly.

"What?"

"How many crew members still believe the Tsosa is a myth?"

"Practically everyone."

"How many want him off the ship?"

"Are you joking?"

"Where are Jan and the Mar Vin now?" Ma shot.

"Her compartment."

"Get ten crew members in here before she returns, Dak, and we will end this."

"Mutiny?"

"The Mar Vin is an imposter," Ma said, "and it seems So Jan has been captivated by him. This is not mutiny. We are acting in the best interests of the crew and the mission of the To. We cannot just sit here. This is a battle cruiser. We must get back into the action, for the Яω, for Roi Tan, for ourselves."

"Aye."

"Hurry, Dak."

"Aye."

Ma smiled openly as Dak left the bridge. "Did you get all that?" she asked.

"Yes," άl Ebon's voice thundered through her mind.

"What do you want me to do now?"

"Kill them both."

"Aye."

"Is the Cobalt bomb still aboard the To?" ál Ebon asked.

"In silo seven."

"Armed?"

"Aye."

"Send that missile into the United Nations Space Corps headquarters in Atlantae."

"In the infra-red spectrum?"

"Any color spectrum will do."

"Aye," Ma said gallantly.

"Aye," ál Ebon mimicked. He could not help himself and he laughed aloud.

"But I do not know how to…"

"Someone will teach you, Ma."

"Who?"

"His name is Josh. He will contact you."

"When?'

"He is quite busy right now. Soon."

"What can I do in the meantime?"

"Secure your ship."

"Are you open to an idea, Master?"

"I'm listening."

"I can duplicate the gel chip you implanted in me…"

"Jan?"

"Yes."

"Do it."

* * *

Marvin pulled at the sleeves of an ill fitting shirt which had been provided by someone in the crew at Jan's request. With his arms nearly splitting the sleeves, he forced it across his chest.

"We have never had a man on this ship," Jan said with a smile. "But you'd think someone would know how to measure for a shirt." She leaned back against the bulkhead and closed her eyes. In a few moments she returned to reality and leaned on an elbow. "We will not be able to help Tan at Penumbra, Mar Vin."

"Even so, the alternative can be just as devastating."

"To attack ὰl Ebon."

"Yes."

"In his stronghold."

"Yes."

"Never been done."

"That's why it's possible."

"Яω told you?"

Marvin ignored the question. "I want to recover my weapon from the lake. It shouldn't take long," he said.

"Why?"

"I'll need it later."

"It cannot compare to our technology."

"It's good for killing."

"It's primitive."

"Yes."

"I don't understand."

"Just call it a back-up."

* * *

Marvin had been gone for only a few moments when Dak burst into Jan's quarters, her side arm charged and looking for blood. Backed by Uni Tau Pax and several lower ranking crew members, all of whom seemed ill at ease, Dak assumed command of the room and bullied Jan immediately. She was unconcerned about any disquieting feelings among the crew for what she was about to do.

"The buffoon," she screamed at Jan, jerking at her clothing. "Where is he?"

"Buffoon?" Jan asked sarcastically. "Do you see a buffoon?"

"Your weapon?"

"Find it yourself."

"You are detained, So Jan." Dak barked.

She turned to one of the junior officers. "Tell So Ma that Jan has been detained but that we have not found the Mar Vin."

"Ma, again," Jan said quietly. "Who promoted her to So?"

"You… when you stuck that pathetic human in the ReCon chamber and called him the Tsosa, for allowing him to enter the bridge and for mating with him."

"Ma is an άl Ebon operative."

"Shut up!"

"You have been duped."

"Shut…"

"She will order you to kill me…"

"Shut…"

"…and Mar Vin."

Dak smashed the butt of her weapon into Jan's forehead and watched the person who had been her commander for over two centuries crumple onto the floor, with a great deal of satisfaction.

"I told you…" she said, as she spun on the ball of one foot, "…to shut up!" Dak screamed into the face of one of the nearest officers, "Find the Mar Vin!" She looked back at Jan and sneered. "And secure this room until So Ma decides what to do with this feckless, gullible, washed out traitor."

"Stand guard," she shot at Pax. "Look everywhere," she commanded the others around her as she moved into the passageway outside the compartment.

When Dak had gone, Pax gently pulled the unconscious Jan back onto her bed. "I'm so sorry," she whispered, "I know something is wrong, but I don't know what to do about it."

She covered Jan and moved just outside the compartment door but could not bring herself to lock it. Pulling her weapon, she checked its available power and, for a reason unknown to her, cocked it, concealing the fact that it was ready to fire. Pax stood with arms crossed, her finger resting gently against the trigger, trying to decide what action she would take if Ma and Dak actually made a move to kill Jan. She listened to members of the crew rummage through nearby compartments looking for the Mar Vin and leaned back into the bulkhead with a resigned face.

"Ma may have taken charge of the To but she is not the leader Jan was," Pax thought. *"How many members of the crew would actually follow Ma if she tried to lead them into battle? The ship will be powering up to launch and, sadly, there does not seem to be a lot of time to act,"* she thought, *"Something convincingly positive needs to occur quickly, or a grave mistake is likely to be made."*

Pax had almost decided to reenter Jan's compartment when a voice seemed to come alive from deep within her brain. *"Jan?"* the voice said urgently. *"Jan!"* it repeated.

Pax spun, thinking someone in the passageway had spoken and walked to the nearest hatch. She saw no one and returned to her post. *"Jan,"* the voice called again. *"What is wrong? Why are you not responding?"*

"Because she is unconscious," Pax thought to herself.

"Unconscious!" the voice demanded.

"She has been detained by Ma," Pax spoke aloud, almost involuntarily. *"Ma,"* she thought again.

"ǻl Ebon." The voice communicated with a clear certainty.

"Who are you?" Pax demanded aloud. Shaken, she was suddenly convinced that something frighteningly powerful had taken control of her mind. Functioning arbitrarily and without her consent, it was moving her thoughts dangerously close to sedition. Was a real voice speaking to her?

"No," she thought, *"Something is really wrong and I am about to lose control of my mind. I must get to ReCon."*

As she turned to leave her post, the voice spoke again. *"Who is this?"* it asked.

"Pax. I am Pax," she screamed, holding her ears to prevent the voice from continuing.

"Pax," the voice said calmly, *"I am Marvin. Please help me."*

Pax, moving at a fast pace, had just entered the passageway leading to ReCon, her hand was reaching for the compartment door when she came up short. "The Mar Vin?" she asked.

"Marvin. Yes. What has happened to So Jan?"

She was prevented from answering when someone opening the door from inside moved abruptly into the passageway. *"Ma!"* Pax thought, as the So whisked past, heading for the bridge and leaving the door standing open behind her for Dak to close as she marched away with a frustrated look on her face.

"Yes, I am working as fast as I can," Ma said to no one as she moved beyond hearing.

"Even she is talking to herself," Pax thought.

Pax pulled the compartment door toward her and leaned her back into it, relieved.

She realized she still had a loaded weapon in her hand and shook her head in disbelief, embarrassed. After resetting the safety, she shoved it forcefully into its holster and turned back toward her station outside Jan's compartment. As she walked, Pax came to the conclusion that even if everything were wrong, the voice inside her head was proof somehow of a ship-wide dysfunction, probably the computer, simply a manifestation of the chaos around her. She felt herself again and was relieved.

"Pax," the voice said. *"You must hurry."*

"Go away!" Pax shot.

"ál Ebon will order her killed or worse."

"I am not listening."

"Let me back into the ship."

"You're outside the ship?"

"I can help Jan. Let me in."

"No."

"Ma is an ál Ebon operative. She has already tried to kill Jan and would have succeeded if I had not shot her. Jan thought she had cleared away Ma's link to ál Ebon when Ma was rehabilitated in the ReCon chamber but that seems not to have worked, because Ma is at it again. Too much is at stake, Pax. Let me in."

"You shot Ma?"

"Yes."

"How?"

"With the weapon I am now holding in my hand."

"What kind of weapon?"

"A primitive human weapon."

"…before you became the Tsosa."

"I am not the Tsosa. But we will find the Tsosa today if you will just let me in."

"How do I know you are telling me the truth?"

"Ask Jan."

"Unconscious."

"Maybe that should tell you something."

"Where are you?"

"Outside the aft loading dock."

"I can't leave Jan."

"Can you trust anyone?"

"Yes."

"...anyone still loyal to Jan?"

"Yes."

"Have one of them let me in."

"Let me think about it."

CHAPTER TWENTY

SEPTEMBER 4, 2002
THE BONEYARD

Josh, moving at blazing speed, almost too fast for the human eye to follow, had re-written over ten-thousand pages of code, blending the forces of ál Ebon into an overwhelmingly unified and terrifying force, aimed at one specific target in the solar system and directly under the command of but one voice, his Master's. Then, having detailed every nuance of the newly written code, Josh was not surprised when the Master did not ask for a single revision. After having completed his last assignment within minutes of his estimated time frame, Josh moved his chair to the center of his console and quietly awaited his Master's command.

"Everything is ready," Josh said.

"Attack," ál Ebon said without hesitation, his voice echoing through the entire complex.

"Yes, Master," Josh said as he sharply pushed a button at the heart of his console.

"Travel time?"

"28.21 hours, Master."

"Is that to the face of the moon or the city of Penumbra?"

"Penumbra."

"Very good, Josh... Josh?"

"Yes, Master."

"Thank you for your service."

"You are welcome, Master."

"Someone will be along to separate you from the chair."

As he said this, three young technicians, wearing only tight fitting white denim coveralls without pockets, but emblazoned with an ál Ebon logo across the back, arrived, pushing a massive red tool chest that squeaked thunderously as one of its wheels skidded sideways, jittering across the smoothly troweled, lime-green cement floor.

Josh wondered, as they went about their work, what it might have been like to have experienced life with an entire body, or to have been able to move from place to place at will, or to have experienced the world outside his cubicle, and he was overwhelmed by a sense of loss. Then, realizing he could not imagine anything outside the walls of his cubicle, Josh was calmed. He had simply experienced another kind of life and he was somehow satisfied by that thought.

The technicians did not speak to themselves or to Josh, as they began disassembling his chair from the back in order to reach his spinal cord and, as one of the young women worked, Josh experienced a wrenching sensation but no pain as his body was disconnected from the system. When free, he was placed across a rolling gurney and his head carefully disconnected from the circuits connecting him to the fleet, leaving a crown covering his skull of a thin alloy into which the circuits had been plugged.

Josh immediately felt an enormous sense of loss. He could no longer hear the voice of his Master, nor receive digital feedback from a thousand drones, and he felt a swell of self pity as the gurney was pulled unceremoniously from his cubicle and pushed rapidly into the long corridor which intersected thousands of cubicles just like his.

A strange and unexpected thing happened as Josh was being removed from the complex. All of the drone-interface specialists on his floor clicked their fingertips against their consoles in salute as he passed by. The quiet sound was a roar. The sweeping disappointment left him, replaced by an overwhelming feeling of comradeship for people he had never known, would never see and to whom he would never speak. He could still hear the clicking long after he had been pushed though an aircontainment lock and lay waiting for a large rolling door to be raised, so that he could be removed from the complex.

Outside, Josh was immediately blinded by sunlight. The intense heat of desert air burned his lungs as he inhaled and he tried to move just a few inches to the side, so he could get his face under the shadow of the awning. A technician misunderstood his intentions and caught him, holding Josh in place by placing a hand on Josh's chest and pushing down hard.

"Ever been to the boneyard?" he asked his companion.

"Uh uh," the second technician said.

The men remained on the loading dock with Josh until a large construction drone pounded its way out of the service center from the north side of the complex and squatted into the dock, ventilating a foul smelling steam from exhausts along its sides and stretching out long, spider-like legs which bent surprisingly gracefully at the knees as the machine settled. A long arm reached from its freight bay and snatched Josh's body from the gurney with opposable thumb-like claws and Josh experienced pain for the first time in his life as the drone deposited him unceremoniously into the bay, pushing him into a corner with several other drone-interface specialists who had already died.

For half an hour, the drone moved around the outside of the complex from dock to dock, picking up retired specialists. Most were dead but a few were in the process of dying and cried piteously as their half-bodies were stacked clumsily against the back wall of the drone's bay. When the drone had made its final pick-up, it lifted into the sky with such force that tears filled Josh's eyes. The machine moved rapidly across the desert and within minutes arrived at a long wadi which, years before, had been converted into an open graveyard, the stagnant smell of decaying flesh filling the lifeless desert air for miles in every direction.

Since Josh had been among the first loaded, he wound up on top of the pile as bodies of the specialists were scraped from the bay by the claw. Then, within seconds, he was finally alone in an unbearable heat that seemed to cook him from the inside out and he wanted to scream. Before this moment, he had never entertained any notions about the act of dying but he could see that those around him had breathed their last before being dumped in this place and it seemed a good thing that they had. Death was all around him. For the others, death had been a blessing. For him, it was torture.

Josh feebly raised an arm to block the sun, a thing he had experienced so long ago as pleasurable, a thing he had nearly forgotten existed, a thing which now burned his skin and made him wish death would come soon. The desert was quiet except for a low wind which moved dust and small particles of sand in tiny swirling eddies that danced among the corpses. Occasionally, an eddy passed over Josh, filling his eyes with grit before moving on. Josh worked hard to free himself from the blistering sun and the dancing dust devils and eventually found himself turned completely over with his face pressed into the back of one of the specialists who had been delivered with him to this place.

Even though Josh now found it difficult to breathe, he preferred being face down and he relaxed into the experience of dying.

On his stomach, Josh was unable to know that a second drone had come racing across the desert from the complex an hour later and hovered above the bodies in the wadi. It began to search for something, moving slowly back and forth above the boneyard scanning faces and reporting to ál Ebon. Because Josh's back was now turned to the sun, the drone, purposed by ál Ebon to find and return him to the complex, was forced to carefully scan tens of thousands of bodies as it attempted to complete its task and the more it scanned, the further away from Josh it moved.

CHAPTER TWENTY ONE

SEPTEMBER 4, 2002
A KILLING SPREE

In unison, the grays began to whine as Dak worked her way through the cruiser, killing members of the crew she believed loyal to Jan. The unarmed died quickly, littering the forward compartments, as she cleared each space all the way back to the bridge. Grays bumped into each other as she worked, ignoring them. Hysterically, they ran in all directions, trying to hide from the chaos. One of them alerted Pax that something had turned dreadfully wrong, when it scurried past her, turned abruptly and, eluding Pax, entered Jan's compartment only to slide under the bed, a place where it might be safe.

"What is happening?" Pax said aloud. She began to hear a weapon firing and the ensuing commotion in the forward compartments and stepped closer to the nearest hatch, listening.

"What is it?" the voice inside her head begged immediately.

"I don't know," she thought.

"Oh, my God!" the voice suddenly shouted.

"What?"

"Dak is killing everyone."

"Don't be absurd!"

"I can hear their dying screams. Pax...LET ME IN!"

"I can't leave So Jan."

"Carry her!"

"I..."

"Now!"

"Aye," Pax said, her voice filled with an unexpected resolve.

"Bring everyone you can find aft with you!"

"Aye."

Pax moved through the opened door and into Jan's compartment, immediately looking under the bed. "You must carry her," she said to the gray, who began to give out a high-pitched whine. Pax pulled the bed away from the bulkhead and wrenched the gray up by the arm with one hand while she yanked her weapon from its holster, aiming it at the gray's face. In a state of shock, the gray remained frozen, unwilling to move, and Pax was unwilling to argue the point. She had begun charging her weapon when the gray finally made its choice and, moving to the bed, effortlessly lifted Jan onto its shoulder. Without waiting, it started for the door, where it turned to go forward.

"No," Pax shouted. "Aft, to the loading dock."

* * *

Dak had worked her way all the way back to the corridor leading to the bridge and, with a murderous look on her face, burst through the door in time to hear the last of a one-sided conversation between Ma and ál Ebon. Dak's expression changed to disbelief as the meaning of what she could hear became clear to her and she audibly sucked in her breath. Although Ma's back was to Dak as she talked, Ma was well aware of the other's presence and could feel the disbelief oozing from her junior officer. Ma removed her weapon from its holster and levered the charge mechanism, knowing what was to come. Dak had been fooled and she had one hell of a temper.

"It will take some time to replicate the gel implants, Master."

Ma listened.

"The crew is being killed now."

Ma listened.

"In cold storage."

Ma listened.

"Yes, Master, they can be revived later."

Ma listened."

"Dak and I will be able to handle the cruiser by ourselves, Master."

Ma listened.

"No, Master, she has not found the Tsosa."

"What have I done?" Dak cried as she clumsily worked at recharging her weapon. Too late, Ma spun and fired just as Dak's weapon came on line and the Uni Tau was slammed backward, through the open doorway and out into the passage beyond, where she slid into a small pile and died with a shocked look on her face that remained as her body slumped onto the deck.

Ma listened once more.

"No, Master. I cannot trust any of the remaining crew. I will have to seal off the bridge and proceed by myself.

Ma listened one final time.

"Yes, Master," she said.

Ma immediately began sealing off the main deck aft of the bridge. When she was confident that no one would breach her security measures, she began re-writing codes that would allow her to reassign command tasks to herself, obviating the need for So Jan's voice commands or Personal Command Number. It would take hours, but άl Ebon had committed his fleets to a final solution at Penumbra and it was now up to her to disrupt the command and control of Roi Tan's forces by destroying the UNSC's underwater headquarters in Atlantae.

As she worked, Ma gloated. She was in the process of re-writing history. The To's electronic signature would fool the Aegis at Atlantae, allowing the cruiser to glide into port without providing the necessary security codes. Oh yes, the destruction of Atlantae had nearly been accomplished thousands of years earlier by a much weaker άl Ebon, but now it would be her turn. With an armed Cobalt bomb buried inside the missile in silo 7, she would drive the To into Atlantae and change everything with a single, definitive blow.

άl Ebon was hours away from destroying the vaunted United Nations Space Corps at Penumbra and she would follow up at Atlantae, an unbeatable one-two combination of destruction, victory and glory. άl Ebon would rule forever and Яω would quickly become a distant memory.

CHAPTER TWENTY TWO

SEPTEMBER 4, 2002
THE DOOR TO RECON IS SEALED FROM THE OUTSIDE

With a still unconscious Jan, six frightened low-grade U Chi crew-members and four grays, Uni Tau Pax reached the aft loading dock in somewhat of a panic. In her haste to open the hatch, there seemed to be the possibility that it would not release and she yanked desperately at the lever, forgetting that a simple four digit code needed to be entered into a release mechanism before the hatch could be activated and she lost her temper in frustration. A gray reached around her, quietly punching in the correct number sequence and the door immediately swung outward with a great whoosh.

The heady, rich aroma of damp forest filled her nostrils and far in the background, over the ragged top of a distant mountain, the sun had begun setting, splaying reds and golds across a deep blue sky behind the Mar Vin as he came aboard carrying something Pax had never before seen – a rifle. Pax was surprised once again by his size and starred in amazement at the monster of a man as he worked his way across the outside hull of the cruiser and stepped gracefully inside.

Dwarfed by his presence, Pax backed away as the hatch was

resealed, trying to achieve some psychic distance from Marvin, knowing instinctively, now that she was in his presence, that he was indeed the Tsosa and she went to her knees, with all of the crew members following suit except for the grays, who milled uneasily in the far side of the dock, mewling softly.

Marvin immediately knelt by Jan's side, cupping the back of her head in his enormous hand. "What happened to her?" he asked, almost academically. He did not wait for an answer but picked Jan up and turned toward Pax. "How do we get to the bridge from here?" he asked.

"It has been sealed off," Pax said.

"Ma."

"No one can get past the conflagration doors now that they have been secured. Getting to the bridge is an impossibility."

"Do you have weapons?" Marvin asked.

"Aye," Pax said.

In unison, all of the crew members pulled their weapons from their holsters. Clearly distraught, the grays cringed and backed into a corner, whining loudly.

"Charge your weapons."

"Aye."

"Now get us to a computer that can override anything that is being written on the bridge."

"I'm not sure that is possible," Pax said.

"Think," Marvin demanded.

"It may be…" Pax thought aloud, "the computer in ReCon… but I don't know…"

"Get us there."

"Aye."

"And bring my rifle."

Pax led the way as all of the crew members followed closely with Marvin a few steps behind, carrying Jan. The grays did not come. Within a few meters, Pax opened a door and went inside a storage compartment assigned to the grays, looking for another survivor. When satisfied the room was empty, she returned to the corridor and the small caravan continued. She did this several times until the group had reached a ladder which would take them up to the main deck.

At the top of the ladder, the door was closed and she turned to Marvin, looking past the crew. "We have to go through this door…" she said quietly.

Marvin sat Jan on the floor and gently slapped her face. When she responded, he shook her shoulders and she came awake with a gasp. "What…" she said groggily and her arms reached up to encircle Marvin's neck. "You're here," she said.

"Ma was right," Pax cried in astonishment. "You did bed him!" She pointed her weapon toward Jan, but could not bring herself to fire. So Jan had broken the cardinal rule of leadership. She had had knowledge of a man and must be punished, but Pax could not think of how punishment might be administrated in this crisis and relented. The weapon dropped to her side and her eyes welled with tears.

"Now is not the time for this," Marvin said. "I will go first." He pulled Jan's arms from around his neck and moved toward Pax, who did nothing to stop him. Marvin gently took the rifle from her hand, opened the breech to inspect it and slammed the bolt home, pushing a live round into the chamber. When he moved to climb the ladder, Pax followed closely.

“I will follow you, Mar Vin,” she said quietly.

At the top of the ladder, Marvin stood, undecided as to how to proceed. He did not want to break through the door and into a trap, nor did he want to be shot by a frightened survivor and he turned to Pax with a perplexed look on his face.

“Maybe you ought to go first,” he said. “Someone might not be so apt to take a shot at you.”

“Aye,” Pax said bravely and squeezed past Marvin without reservations.

She gently opened the door wide enough to look into the corridor. When convinced that no one was there, she leaned into the door and went to her knees with the weapon just in front of her face. As the door swung open, she encountered another Uni Tau named Sol, who had pushed her body against the wall just behind the door and was ready to kill in her own defense.

“Pax!” she screamed silently, gratefully.

“Is there anyone else?” Pax asked as she moved into the corridor with Marvin close behind.

Sol was trembling so hard she could barely answer. “I don’t think so,” she whispered. “There are several grays, though.”

“Where is Dak?”

“I haven’t seen her since the conflagration doors were sealed.”

“Is ReCon empty?”

“Yes. Two Uni Tau’s are in the chambers. No one else is there.”

“Good,” Marvin said. “Let’s move.”

Pax pushed her way into ReCon with her weapon in front of her face and when the room was found to be empty, motioned and everyone quickly scurried in behind her. Jan was beginning to think clearly and she showed Marvin how to access the main frame from the ReCon's auxiliary computer.

Marvin began entering strings of commands without even looking at the screen and within a very short period of time, the lights went off in the compartment, the lids to both ReCon chambers popped open and Pax could hear systems shutting down all across the ship.

"What did you do?" she demanded.

"He's shut down the mainframe," Jan said.

"We'll need some light," Marvin said.

"Our weapons," Jan said. "Click the first setting."

"Check the people inside the chambers," Marvin said.

"I will," Sol said and she leaned into the first one. "Still asleep," she reported. "Both are still asleep," she said a minute later.

"Stay with them," Marvin said. "If they wake, see if they can handle a weapon."

"Aye."

"Ma will know where we are," Jan said.

"Can we open the conflagration doors from this station?" Marvin asked.

"I think so…" Jan said. "…but the main frame is down," she added quietly.

"I think I can access the upper memory without starting it up again," Sol said confidently.

"How will you get power?" Jan asked.

"There is a back-up power supply station for the ReCon

chambers," Sol continued. "It's in a compartment next to the aft loading dock."

At that moment, the power was restored, the lights came on and systems throughout the ship began coming on line again. Marvin leapt to the computer and was furiously entering code when Sol left the compartment.

"I won't be a minute," she said.

"What is Sol's area of specialty?" Marvin asked when she was gone.

"Weapons," Jan said. "Her assigned station is the armory."

Sol stood in front of the closed door to the lab for long moments, considering. Finally she turned toward the conflagration doors instead of the ladder which would take her to the lower decks, moving quickly. At the conflagration doors, she waited before pulling the shipboard communicator from its wall socket and made her call to Ma.

"Jan and the Mar Vin are in the ReCon lab," Sol said.

"I know," Ma said.

"Pax is with them."

"Good. How many crew members are with you?"

"None…at the moment."

"Where is everyone?"

"In the compartment adjacent to the aft loading dock."

"Where are you?"

"Still on the main deck near the conflagration doors."

"Why did you come here?"

"I thought you might need help."

"No. Is everyone in the aft compartment armed?"

"Aye."

"Good."

"And Ma?" Sol said. "So Jan and the Mar Vin have known each other."

"It was foretold."

"What does that mean?"

"They must die!"

Sol was silent for a long moment.

"They must never again be able to gain access to a ReCon station," Ma said.

Sol remained silent.

"Can you do this, Sol?"

"Aye."

"Then seal the door to ReCon from the outside. I will do the rest."

"I thought you said…"

"I will terminate the air supply to the main deck. Once you have sealed the door, return to the aft compartment by the loading dock and let me know you have completed your task."

"Aye."

Sol locked the communicator back into its wall socket and walked aft, toward the ladder which would return her to the lower decks, but as she was about to pass the ReCon lab she paused, thinking, and instead of continuing on, gingerly opened the door to the lab with one hand and entered with a charged weapon in the other.

As the door opened, Pax pulled her weapon but was shot where she stood. Sol quickly placed her weapon on the floor and, raising her hands, looked straight into the Mar Vin's eyes. "Ma wants you sealed inside this compartment so she can eliminate you by terminating the air supply to this deck," she said, without taking a breath.

"I wondered where you stood," Marvin said. "Do you know anything about upper memory?"

"No."

"What do you recommend, Uni Tau Sol?"

"We seal the door to this compartment and tell Ma when my mission has been accomplished."

"And?"

"You move to the lower decks until the conflagration doors have been opened."

"Aye," Jan said. "But what about the people in the chambers?

"Take them with you."

"Aye," Jan said again.

Sol starred at Jan for a long moment. "You have broken the rules, So Jan," she said sadly.

The lights went out again. The ship was silent throughout.

* * *

With the unconscious crew members pulled from the ReCon Chambers, and all the grays they could find on the main deck, Jan and Marvin slowly worked their way through the dark corridors and into the aft loading dock where they waited for Sol to report that the conflagration doors had been opened. Sol, in the meantime, melted the door of the ReCon lab to its jamb and then destroyed the locking device with a final burst of her weapon.

CHAPTER TWENTY THREE

SEPTEMBER 4, 2002
KILLING RANJOSHITEÉ

"It is done," Sol said.

Ma pushed the bridge communicator back into its cradle with a deliberate vengeance. Her victory complete, she reveled in her hard earned triumph. "Done," she cried. She was actually going to kill the Tsosa and destroy the disgusting diatribe which had haunted Indus for thousands of years; she was going to annihilate Ranjoshiteé, a nauseating little worm who had somehow been transformed into a fearsome goddess of war because no one had been strong enough to challenge her and she was going to obliterate Atlantae and all its meaning to a gullible, whining, corrupt culture.

Glory was hers.

ál Ebon would rule for eternity, from this moment on, now and forever, and the name Ma would live eternally in the hearts and minds of the people of Indus, a goddess herself. And she will have singlehandedly destroyed the one thing ál Ebon could not: Atlantae.

Ma threw her head back and laughed until tears filled her eyes. She jabbed at the button which would expel oxygen from the main deck into the atmosphere surrounding the ship and stared at her finger.

"One little finger," she thought. *"One little finger is destroying every hope, every prediction. Ranjoshiteé... you little grub, die!"*

She sat in the So's chair and, using one foot to propel herself in circles, spun through the bridge until she was exhausted. Ma walked to the control console and jabbed the button again and again. When she had composed herself, Ma opened the hatch from the bridge to the outside of the ship and stood on one of the wide, flat, port nacelles, deeply breathing the aromas of the forest, watching the air from the main deck vent itself out in gossamer streams all along the sides of the ship.

An hour later, she went inside and closed the hatch and picked up the communicator.

"It has been done," Sol reported to Ma as the lights inside the ship came on once again.

"You have done well," Ma said. "You are now my second in command, Sub So Sol. Once I have confirmed that Jan and the Mar Vin have been eliminated, I want you to share the moment with me when they drag the bodies off this ship."

"Aye."

"Where are you now?"

"With the crew in the aft locker."

"And the door to the main deck is sealed?"

"Aye."

"When they are dead, I will meet you at the door to ReCon."

"Aye."

Sol pushed the communicator into its cradle and turned to the remaining crew members of the pocket cruiser To. "Ma has sold out to ál Ebon," she said. "She has continually tried to kill So Jan and failed and the Mar Vin is truly the Tsosa. The prediction has become a reality and we are in the throes of change. In this moment, we cannot afford to err."

Ma made one last call to Sol, unable to hide the joy in her voice. "We need to open the door to the ReCon lab," she said.

"Aye," Sol said

"Bring everyone with you. You will need some help carrying the bodies."

"Aye."

So Ma and Sub So Sol stood to the side while five crew members worked furiously at opening the lab door. When it had finally been pried free, Ma pushed everyone aside. Victory was hers and she would open the door – but when she stepped into the compartment, it was completely empty and she spun on the ball of one foot and glared at Sol.

"You lied," Ma breathed wickedly.

"They were here! You know it yourself. They were here."

Ma pulled her weapon and the remaining crew members followed suit.

"Where?" she demanded.

"They could not get through the conflagration doors and they could not remain on the main deck. The aft loading dock! They could only be in the aft loading dock."

Ma studied Sol for a long moment and then she smiled. "Yes, of course," she said. "Give me your weapon."

Without reservation, Sol handed her weapon to Ma, butt first.

"I'm sorry," she said.

"Lead the way," Ma said in an even voice. Once or twice, she jabbed Sol in the back as they proceeded down to the aft loading dock.

Ma stood for a long moment, deliberating with herself before she spoke in a menacing voice to her crew. "When this door is open, you will fire into this compartment until everyone inside is dead."

When the firing had ceased, Ma entered the room and kicked at every body, turning each, cursing. At last, she turned to her crew.

"Grays!" she screamed. "You've killed all the grays!"

"You haven't recharged your weapon," Sol said calmly.

One of the crew members handed her weapon to Sol and she fired point blank into Ma's face.

CHAPTER TWENTY FOUR

SEPTEMBER 4, 2002
THE 'AL EBON DRONE-INTERFACE

A lone drone raced across the Gobi, close to the floor of the desert, kicking up sand and dust as it sped along. Within moments it arrived at the graveyard of discarded drone-interfaces controlled by a single mission: gather the body of Josh and, if it was still alive, return it to the complex where it would be resuscitated and returned to service. Never before had the Master ordered such a mission. Never before had ál Ebon experienced second thoughts about anything. This was his first exception and it would follow a choice he would live to regret.

"A single drone is traveling at high speed across the surface of the planet," the computer reported.

"Unusual," Jan said, almost to herself. "Can you identify its destination?"

"It has arrived at its destination," the computer reported.

"Identify."

"It is a place where tens of thousands of bodies have been deposited."

"A graveyard?"

"You must land there," Marvin said.

"None of the bodies have been buried," the computer reported.

"Plot a landing solution adjacent to that location."

"A landing solution has been plotted."

"Is the drone aware of our presence?"

"Yes."

"Why has it not turned to attack us?"

"It appears to be on a special mission."

"Can you identify what that might be?"

"It is searching for something."

"We must hurry," Marvin said.

"Plot a firing solution to stun the drone."

"A firing solution has been plotted."

"Fire!" Jan turned to her second-in-command. "Sol, take four crew members. Search this area."

"What will I be looking for?" Sol mused aloud, then looked at Marvin.

Jan also turned to Marvin, an unspoken question on her face.

"We will help you from here," Marvin said. "But you may have to move fast."

* * *

"Can you hear me?" a voice asked.

Josh was stunned. For years, he had only heard the thoughts of άl Ebon, and the two halves of his mind collided: the rational, for sorting and disseminating outgoing information to hundreds of robot drones and the irrational, for receiving and decoding millions of kilobytes per minute of incoming data. He could barely remember the sound of a clear-spoken voice heard through his ears, only the cacophony of thousands as they communicated with the Master simultaneously.

The sound of a single voice was a delicious sensation and his joy was so profound, he became unable to respond.

"Can you hear me?" the voice said again.

"Hello," Josh said tentatively. His mind raced. Was he hallucinating?

"Who are you?" the voice said.

"J-Josh."

"Where are you, Josh?"

"Within my mind and body."

"I see. Where is that?"

"Here."

"Thank you. Where is the Master?"

"The Master is everywhere."

"Do you know the Master, Josh?"

"Very well."

"Why are you here, Josh?"

"I have been discarded."

"Discarded?"

"Yes, I am at the end of my life cycle."

"Discarded?"

"I have been brought here to die."

There was a long silence where no one spoke.

"I have reached the limit of my usefulness," Josh clarified.

"What do you do that is useful, Josh?"

"I am a drone-interface for ál Ebon."

"Oh, my God!" Jan whispered.

"This… is the Tsosa," Marvin said. "Josh… move so we can find you."

"Get him into ReCon," Jan commanded. "NOW!"

* * *

Jan and Marvin stood over Recon One as Josh was gently loaded into the apparatus. With the lid snugly closed, the machine chugged into the enormity of its task as it initialized its first sequence by beginning a cytological examination of Josh. The ship's computer ground to a slow walk, just as it had when Marvin was reconstructed.

"I can't trust him," Jan said as the battle cruiser's systems began to shut down.

"Yes…" Marvin said, "you can."

"He can say anything. Who is to know?"

"He has no moral compass. He has never been asked to make choices."

"And just what does that mean?"

"He is very much like the machine to which he was attached."

"What does that mean?"

"He is amoral, callow, guileless, untouched by culture or ideology."

"You are saying that he could tell us much."

"Yes."

"He can still lie, can't he?"

"That is not possible."

"How do you know?"

"Яω told me."

Jan gasped. "Яω?" she whispered.

"He spoke to me the entire time I was in your ReCon apparatus."

"I thought he was dead. It's been so long."

"Quite the contrary."

"He has asked nothing of me for over four hundred years."

"You were in place. He needed you to be here, at the right moment. The moment is now."

Jan searched his face, trying to discover the truth. "And you?" she asked.

"My job is to provide clarity."

"Why you?"

"I am very much like you, Ranjoshiteé, but whereas you think strategically, have courage and a commitment of will, I have the extraordinary abilities to remember and to calculate."

"You know my name?"

"Яω told me everything."

"What do you know about me?"

"Everything."

"What else did he tell you, Mar Vin."

Marvin was silent.

"Is there more?"

Marvin remained silent.

"Mar Vin?"

"We will have children."

Jan gasped once more. "But I am ugly," she said after a while.

"Well, you saw me."

"How old are you, Mar Vin?"

"Thirty four."

"I am over seven hundred years old, Mar Vin."

"I suppose that is unimportant."

"We would have ugly children."

"No."

"No?"

"At this moment, both our bodies and minds are functioning nearly perfectly."

"I have never made love with anyone."

CHAPTER TWENTY FIVE

SEPTEMBER 4, 2002
JOSH EXPLAINS THE UNIVERSE

"ál Ebon is not a person, rather it is a dynastic title," Josh began. "No one outside of his immediate family knows the Master's name and no one knows his immediate family, yet they control solar systems throughout the galaxy.

"To illustrate, let me begin by describing the solar system in terms with which you may not be familiar. It is commonly believed that the system is static and has always remained this way: Mercury, Venus, Earth, etc., all in a row, within unique orbits, circling endlessly, until the sun becomes extinct.

"This picture is inaccurate and naïve. One must take into account the history of the solar system in order to know the Master, remembering that ál Ebon is only one of an eons-long line of sovereigns who have ruled in this tiny sliver of the galaxy. Think of it this way: Seventy five million years ago, his great-great grandfather ruled the ál Ebon dynasty from what is now known as the planet Mars.

"At that time, Mars occupied the orbit of what many now refer to as that of the planet Earth, and Mercury had yet to come into existence. You see, the solar system is not made up of planets revolving in static rings of concentric circles at all. Instead, every planet gradually swirls outward in something like a spiral. An extreme example of this would be that the last body in the current system, now known as Pluto, once occupied the Earth's orbit. When a planet has screwed itself far enough away from the sun, it becomes uninhabitable once more, uncontrolled, combustible. Internal gasses begin to expand its shape: Saturn, Jupiter, Neptune.

"Finally, the system itself is comprised not only of the known planets but also of a line of orbiting bodies strung far out into outer space, all of which once occupied the earth's current orbit. Eventually, with its gasses expended, a planet, like a spent cinder, leaves the influence of the sun's gravitational pull and moves out into space. Now just a rock, it becomes dead space debris, if you will.

"It is only within an orbit like the Earth's that life exists in any solar system, far enough from a sun to be able to capture and hold water being delivered by billions of meteors crashing onto its surface. At this distance from the sun, water and its vapors are reliably protected from the intense heat of the sun and a planet is able to maintain an atmosphere hospitable to life. It is within this tightly controlled orbital environment that the ál Ebon dynasty has existed for millennia. ál Ebon, not the creators of life as some suppose, are merely masters of a dominion, much like your Яω. Neither ál Ebon nor Яω know from which galaxy their lines originated, but both migrated here in another time, from another galaxy. Both claim to be the rightful heirs to this dominion and have been at war with each other since long before Pluto began to circle the sun in its original orbit."

"How do you know these things?" Jan asked.

"I have listened to the thoughts of ál Ebon since I became his subject."

"How do you know that everything you have said is true?"

"Why would ál Ebon lie to himself?" Josh asked.

"Indeed," Marvin said. "How long has ál Ebon existed in this plane?"

"As ál Ebon has done for eons, when the atmosphere of a planet begins to become unstable, the heir to the dynasty moves on with a small contingent, leaving many behind. Incidentally, and for example, those who remained on Mars eventually came under the influence of Яω and in time, formed an alliance with him. Those descendants live there to this day, under harsh conditions, perhaps, but have successfully survived the desert-ification of the planet and the population now thrives as a society with its own unique culture.

"When Earth was first colonized, ál Ebon set about controlling what is now known as Russia. But that icy world was too cold for him and he slowly began to move south and, in time, overcame whole sections of the ancient Indus River. A millennia ago, ál Ebon bullied his way to power over the most influential tribes and, establishing his own religion, proclaimed a 'divine right' to rule and began spreading his belief system and cultural ethic by the sword.

"Emboldened by the inaction of Яω, who had preceded him here, ál Ebon became more and more aggressive. A belligerent, hostile and destructive behavior cowed peaceful, agrarian neighbors, making them reluctant to retaliate, even to protect themselves. Eventually, ál Ebon controlled the entire Indus River Valley, including Harappa.

"With this hub of innovation and commerce under his control, ál Ebon gained a strategic vantage point from which he jealously eyed the entire known world. In an attempt to master every form of waging war, his agents re-acquired the black arts and stealth combat; his clerics, the art of mind control; his alchemists, weapons unknown to man for many millennia to come.

"Eventually, through experimentation, his experts discovered a way to hide from human eyes by manipulating the natural forces around them. He moved from Harappa and settled in the desert, claiming the name Indus for his new home. The people of Indus now existed in the same time and space as their contemporaries on this planet, but remained unseen. When his scientific developments far outpaced the then-known world, one might say ál Ebon became invincible.

"Яω, slow to catch up, had developed a far different culture, manipulating the natural forces around him exactly opposite to ál Ebon. Each became invisible to the inhabitants of the earth and to each other, occupying alternately, the spectrums of light between ultra-violet and infra-red.

"Each created empires, but whereas ál Ebon limited his empire to Earth, Яω spread his kingdom to Mars, Io, Titan and the moon – you call it Penumbra – as well as Earth. He called his dominion Atlantæ and, for hundreds of thousands of years, remained relatively safe from the regressive domination of ál Ebon.

"In time, ál Ebon was able to gain access to the realm of Яω and the real war began. ál Ebon began to attack unarmed merchant freighters of the Confederate Mars Republics in open space. With no governing body to police or even to challenge the aggression, the pirates of ál Ebon rapidly grew in strength. For thousands of years, they attacked private and merchant ships at will throughout the solar system.

"Directing a mindless drone fleet from his unknown location on Earth, ál Ebon eventually targeted all non-combatants and merchant ships from every part of the solar system, destabilizing commerce in the entire region. Hundreds of years ago, all of the trading worlds except Atlantae had declared war against ál Ebon's unseen pirates.

"Eventually, even Atlantæ, with its great Space Corps, was attacked by the robotic gunships of ál Ebon and it too was forced to state publicly that it was at war. In the beginning many, including ál Ebon himself, believed that Atlantæ's powerful United Nations Space Corps could never be defeated. Now, he knows this is not true.

"Even as I speak, ál Ebon has launched a mighty force with the intention of destroying UNSC leadership at Penumbra and its headquarters in Atlantae. Within hours, the great Roi Tan will have been killed and any remaining resistance to ál Ebon will collapse.

"Oddly enough, until now, Яω and ál Ebon have both made half-hearted attempts to rule in the spectrum of light between ultra-violet and infra-red but have been relatively unsuccessful, as humans in this environment are difficult to control. The two warlords have simply produced factions which remain in a constant state of struggle for supremacy. In essence, they have recreated the same enmity experienced in the larger arena, yet have been unable to capitalize on it.

"Now, with the destruction of Atlantæ, ál Ebon will be uncontested in all three spectrums of light."

"The ravings of a lunatic," Jan said.

"You must inform Roi Tan," Marvin said.

"No need, Mar Vin. This eventuality has been anticipated. A trap has been set," Jan said quietly.

CHAPTER TWENTY SIX

SEPTEMBER 5, 2002
PENUMBRA IN THE CROSSHAIRS

The conference ended in the early hours of the morning, and Roi Tan seemed surprisingly discouraged. It had taken much longer for the members of the alliance to come to consensus than she had anticipated, and even though the final vote had been overwhelmingly in favor of her proposals, negotiating to get ambassadors and government heads to agree on even the smallest detail had drained her.

It fell upon her now to reveal to the members of the conference that a massive ál Ebon force would soon attack Penumbra, and preparations to defend against an all-out assault by his drone fleet must get underway.

Off-world members needed to leave immediately, citizens of Penumbra were commanded to man the attack batteries and erect the Aegis, and civilians were encouraged to move to underground bunkers, as there would be no great after-agreement festivities, not even a congratulatory dinner. The force attacking Penumbra would come to destroy everything, kill everyone and reduce a great city to ashes.

Tan raised her arms, asking for silence, but the great hall had come alive with excitement. The festivities were beginning and no one seemed to want to listen further. After all, everything had already been said and the members wanted, more than anything, to enjoy themselves, basking in the glow of victory. An alliance had been forged between and among the most diverse elements of free societies in the solar system without giving up any entrenched, sacred values.

In the past, disagreements over issues large and small had prevented any real discussion, let alone agreement. Roi Tan had finally managed to create a platform which ignored every previous sticking point, and dealt with specific issues, delivering something of value to everyone.

For this, all agreed Tan should be honored and a contingent from Titan soon hoisted her above their heads and began moving slowly through the delegations, after having formed something of a conga line.

Roi Tan's pleas to the crowd to listen were smothered by the revelry. It fell to Sub Roi Bon to communicate with lower grade staff members who began slowly working through the room, informing their leaders of the impending disaster.

Even so, it took nearly an hour for the hall to empty and there were moments of chaos at the docking ports when members of the delegations could not reach their shuttles. More than a few skirmishes between elite guards erupted until all of the delegations had been returned to their ships and made preparations to get underway.

It took hours for Roi Tan to find herself, once again, standing on the bridge of the battle cruiser Ja, after having chosen to remain at the docks until everyone had gotten away safely.

"You look exhausted," Sub Roi Bon said, sympathetically.

Tan ignored the observation and turned her face toward Commander Lawn, the ship's captain. "Have preparations been made to get underway?" she asked.

"Aye."

"Bring all induction drives on line but do not leave this berth," Tan said.

"Aye."

"Computer, report on the progress of the ἁl Ebon fleet," Tan said.

"One hundred forty thousand drones, previously amassing in the upper atmosphere, moved away from the planet en route to Penumbra approximately twenty six hours ago. They will arrive at this location in two hours and seventeen minutes."

"Describe the strategy."

"Attack Penumbra from two sides. Attack the Mars mission while en route."

"Describe the tactics."

"Formations are broken into four clearly defined groups with discrete destinations. Two groups will circle the moon, arriving at Penumbra at the same time. One seems to be held in reserve and the fourth has moved to intercept the Mars delegation. In addition, a small vanguard will reach Penumbra in twelve minutes."

"How small?"

"One thousand drones."

"Inform the Mars delegation."

"A message has been sent," the computer reported one second later.

"Is it possible for them to return to Penumbra?"

"They are too far out," the computer reported.

"Will the drones reach them before they arrive at Mars Station?"

"It will be close," the computer reported.

"This is not good," Tan mused. "Commander Lawn," she ordered,

"Move this ship to the front side of the moon to intercept the incoming ál Ebon fleets."

"Aye."

"Commander Lawn… order the corsairs to attack the vanguard, forcing it to follow us."

"Aye."

"Sub Roi Bon, commit all remaining pocket cruisers to defend the Mars delegation."

"Aye,"

"Sub Roi," Tan said quietly, "accompany me to the ship's armory."

And so, besieged, alone, unprotected by her pocket cruisers and struggling hard to coax uncountable numbers of unrelenting ál Ebon drones to grapple with the Ja at close range, in order to bring the fight to within the Cobalt blast perimeter, Roi Tan slowly maneuvered her crippled battle cruiser around to the far side of the moon, away from Penumbra, and prepared to detonate the Cobalt bomb.

CHAPTER TWENTY SEVEN

SEPTEMBER 5, 2002
THE COBALT BOMB

The To hovered in the stratosphere above the Gobi Desert, directly over the boneyard from which Josh had been recovered. Occupying the spectrum of light between ultra violet and infra red, it remained safely hidden from all ál Ebon sensors. From this position, the ship continuously scanned the planet's surface as it searched for a telltale bloom, which would emanate from any structure consuming massive amounts of electromagnetic input.

Everyone remained expectantly silent while the ship's Aegis began its preliminary report. Twenty seven minutes elapsed. "A massive electromagnetic bloom over the Gobi predicts an enormous complex," the computer reported.

"Is it possible to observe it?" Jan asked.

"Only if the computer plots a spectral reconfiguration solution for the ship which conforms with the spectrum of light being observed," the computer reported.

"Can the exact location of the bloom be pinpointed?"

"The exact location of the bloom has been identified," the

computer reported.

"Plot a landing solution that will take the ship behind the nearest mountain."

"That would be four hundred and fifty four point three miles from the bloom," reported the computer.

"That will not do," Jan mumbled.

"May I suggest a possible solution?" Marvin offered.

"Of course."

"From a distance, say ten miles from the bloom, conform to the infrared spectrum of light and take as many pictures as possible with the gun cameras. If the ship immediately returns to the spectrum of light it currently occupies and then alters its position within seconds, the ál Ebon system might incorrectly identify the signature of the To as a single, unidentifiable blip. It could incorrectly activate a search in the wrong spectrum and in the wrong direction."

"Computer, is that possible?" Jan asked.

"It will take the gun cameras one one-thousandth of a second to recharge after an image has been captured and processed. It will take the gu..."

"Computer, take the ship to within ten miles of the electromagnetic bloom."

"The ship has arrived and is holding in a stationary position at a radius of ten miles from the electromagnetic bloom," the computer reported four minutes later.

"Computer, conform to the infrared spectrum of light for one second, firing all forward and aft gun cameras in every direction for the duration, and return to spectrum of light between infrared and ultra violet, then move to a position directly over the complex."

"Five hundred images from each gun camera have been taken and processed," the computer reported immediately.

"Identify the dimensions of the bloom with a contrast in color and download all pictures to the bridge console," Jan said.

"The download is complete," the computer reported.

Both Jan and Marvin stood transfixed as thousands of individual images flickered across the screen.

"Roi Earn was incorrect," Marvin said.

"Would you classify this as a great city, Mar Vin?" Jan asked.

"Ten miles above the bloom and the To is hovering over at least ten thousand square miles of complex radiating away from the electromagnetic bloom. I would say that qualifies. It may be a good thing that the bloom is situated closer to the edge of the complex."

Marvin paused for a moment. "Over how large an area would one expect the bomb you are carrying on this ship to be effective?" he asked.

"Computer?" Jan said.

"The Cobalt bomb housed within the missile in silo seven will destroy everything, immediately killing any living thing within a forty two point two mile radius. It will render every piece of electronic equipment unusable and permanently disable eighty percent of all living things exposed to the blast within a radius of five hundred seventy five point seven miles. It will…"

Jan turned to Marvin, ignoring the computer. "We can possibly eliminate the bloom and create havoc within a good part of the complex below us," she said in a subdued tone of voice. "But with the bloom existing only above a section of the complex at its outer edge, half of the explosion will be expended in open desert. I was hoping for something a little more definitive."

"The bloom itself must identify the command and control center..." Marvin mused thoughtfully.

"But of the rest?" Jan asked.

"We may have to be satisfied with a reasonable amount of destruction."

"What is reasonable?"

"Eliminate the bloom."

"They can rebuild."

"That is not your issue. Kill the head of the snake."

"Aye," Jan said and she turned back to the computer. "Plot a course around the curvature of the planet that will afford the best protection for the To after the missile carrying the Cobalt bomb has been fired into the section of the complex below us that is defined by the electromagnetic bloom."

"A course has been plotted," the computer reported.

"Target the center of the bloom with the missile in silo seven."

"The target has been selected."

"Set the timing dev..." Jan was interrupted by the computer.

"One hundred drones have been released from the complex and will be within attack distance of the To in one minute forty one seconds," the computer reported.

"Configure the missile's on-board timing devise to explode the cobalt bomb one minute after the missile has penetrated the complex."

"The timing devise has been set," reported the computer.

"Fire the missile in silo seven with instructions to penetrate the complex at the center of the electronic bloom. Alter the ship's spectral configuration to remain within the spectrum of light above infrared. Take evasive action to afford the best protection from the explosion and subsequent radiation of the cobalt bomb."

The To shuddered as the missile was fired.

"The missile in silo seven has been fired," the computer reported. "The ship's spectral configuration now conforms above the infrared spectrum of..." The computer discontinued its report.

"The drone force will be within attack range of the To in one minute six seconds," the computer reported.

CHAPTER TWENTY EIGHT

SEPTEMBER 5, 2002
THE END OF THE BATTLE OF ALL BATTLES

"The Pocket Cruiser To of the United Nations Space Command has just appeared in the atmosphere above Indus," the drone interface said.

"Impossible," ál Ebon said. "Josh reported the To destroyed."

"The Guardian reported sighting the To thirty seconds ago," the drone interface said.

"Thirty seconds?"

"Yes."

Where is it now?"

"I do not know."

"Be specific."

"It was observed for exactly one second, no more and …it has disappeared."

"Ranjoshiteé!"

"Master?"

"It took her long enough!"

"Master?"

"Has Josh been found?"

"No, Master."

"Launch all of the drones of the Indus Guard."

"Yes, Master. Master?"

"Yes."

"The drone sent to find Josh has gone off-line."

ál Ebon was extraordinarily silent for a long moment. "The To is simply in a different spectrum of light," he said at last, almost to himself.

"Yes, Mas…"

"Order my personal drone to be in my courtyard in thirty seconds."

"Master?"

"Twenty eight seconds!"

"Yes, Master."

ál Ebon was airborne when a missile, darting through the sky as if it were an arrow fired from a conjurer's bow, appeared like magic from nowhere and flew unerringly toward the area of the command and control center from which he had just departed. At the speed at which it traveled, the missile flew for mere seconds, but seemed to take an eternity as it ripped through the sky, marking its path with a thin, tight, string of condensation before it punched a neat hole in the roof of the complex.

ál Ebon watched his Indus Guards as their on-board computers triangulated the area from which the missile had been fired. The direction of their search altered a second later as they converged on the place in the sky from which the missile had been launched.

"Too late," ál Ebon mused.

"Identify the nearest mountain range," ál Ebon instructed the onboard computer.

He studied the computer's response for on second. "Land here," he said and placed the tip of a long thin finger on the screen in front of him. Immediately, his craft began moving toward a small mountain range. He thought he would reach safety but when the cobalt bomb detonated, the atmosphere around him rippled violently and the screen on the console of his drone went black.

The drone, no longer under power, now no better than a rock, fell end over end, burying itself in the sand, breaking ál Ebon's spine and knocking him unconscious for the first time in his life, as his ship collapsed around him.

"Ranjoshiteé!" ál Ebon screamed as his drone was captured by the maelstrom.

* * *

At 14:17 on the fifth of September 2002, the entire combat drone fleet of ál Ebon ceased attacking the Ja and began drifting aimlessly: puppets whose strings had been cut. Some forty five years later, they were finally captured by the gravitational pull of the moon and began raining down onto the surface.

At 14:22 on the fifth of September 2002, Roi Tan received a subsonic message from the To:

"Have destroyed άl Ebon command and control, experienced a fierce drone attack and about to crash, located the Tsos..."

BOOKS BY DALE PROCHNOW

Welcome to Idaho

The Tsosa Prophecy

The Tadpole

I Heard the White Wolf Cry

Home of the Hunter

Crosscut

Liberty Call

A Trip to Jerome

The Aestrian Flytrap

Speedway Dreams

The Late Debut of Leighton Lewis

The One True Dictionary

DALE PROCHNOW

Dale Prochnow had a wasted youth. He hot-rodded, shot pool in back rooms of local bars until thrown out, smoked cigarettes, ditched school, got so-so grades (except in English and History), hitchhiked all over the country, and was accused of smearing Limburger cheese on the toilet seats inside the Greyhound Bus Station. He didn't even finish high school.

Did I mention that he was an altar boy?

His Saturdays were spent catching Errol Flynn, Robert Mitchum or Humphrey Bogart in some trashy movie at the Orpheum, craving adventure and loving the dialogue. Foraging through his grammar school library, he discovered a second path to adventure: fiction. Surprised by ideas expressed in the written word, he gobbled up stories like *The Ransom of Red Chief, Thirty Seconds Over Tokyo* and *The Old Man and the Sea*.

Life itself was an experiment. He hocked used cars, bussed tables, fished and hunted, worked in sawmills, sold guns and whiskey, lived through seven months in the South Pacific as a guinea pig for atomic tests, traveled the world, worked for decades as an art director in advertising, and created and marketed bronze statues in galleries throughout the Southwest… all while soaking up how people spoke, dressed, behaved and loved.

His true love has always been telling stories.

www.ingramcontent.com/pod-product-compliance
Lightning Source LLC
LaVergne TN
LVHW010621100826
845148LV00014B/3057

* 9 7 8 1 6 0 7 8 9 3 7 5 2 *